Mollie Hardwick is the author of many historical novels, most recently THE MERRYMAID and GIRL WITH A CRYSTAL DOVE. She is also known to television viewers as the author of the UPSTAIRS DOWNSTAIRS, BY THE SWORD DIVIDED and JULIET BRAVO books. However, she has had a life-long interest in detective fiction, which was responsible for her knowing Dorothy L. Sayers. With her husband Michael Hardwick, she has written many books and plays incorporating Sherlock Holmes.

The Hardwicks live in a fifteenth-century house in Kent, which is also home to two cats, Hudson and Marigold.

Also by Mollie Hardwick

MALICE DOMESTIC

and published by Corgi Books

PARSON'S PLEASURE

Mollie Hardwick

CORGI BOOKS

PARSON'S PLEASURE

A CORGI BOOK   0 552 13236 5

Originally published in Great Britain by
Century Hutchinson Ltd.

PRINTING HISTORY
Century Hutchinson edition published 1987
Corgi edition published 1989

This book is set in Joanna 10/11pt by
Chippendale Type, Otley, West Yorkshire

Corgi Books are published by Transworld Publishers Ltd.,
61 – 63 Uxbridge Road, Ealing, London W5 5SA, in
Australia by Transworld Publishers (Australia) Pty. Ltd.,
15 – 23 Helles Avenue, Moorebank, NSW 2170, and in
New Zealand by Transworld Publishers (N.Z.) Ltd.,
Cnr. Moselle and Waipareira Avenues, Henderson,
Auckland.

Printed and bound in Great Britain by
Cox & Wyman Ltd., Reading, Berks.

CONTENTS

All chapter headings are taken from *The Ingoldsby Legends: or, Mirth and Marvels,* by 'Thomas Ingoldsby Esq.' (the Reverend Richard Harris Barham, 1788-1845).

CHAPTER ONE

Look at the Clock! do! look at the Clock!

'Peace, perfect peace,' Doran murmured, indolently reaching out from the cushioned garden hammock for the tall frosted glass of John Collins on the table beside her.

Rodney, prone in a long garden chair, half opened his eyes.

'Don't speak too soon.'

As she carried the glass to her lips a wasp swooped purposefully down and sat on the rim. She put it down hastily and swiped at the wasp with a book. It appeared to think this some sort of game, dancing away and returning to the rim, where traces of sugar lingered. Rodney watched with amusement.

'Don't thwart it, poor thing – its one ambition is to experience a beautiful death.'

'Not in my drink, it won't.' A violent flourish with the book caught the wasp fair and square; it buzzed angrily off. Doran drank swiftly before it could return with friends. Rodney shut his eyes again.

'It's a natural law, you know,' he mused. 'If you say things like "Peace, perfect peace" in the garden, wasps descend in cohorts. If you say them in the house – like "Isn't it quiet" – the television blows up. I knew a couple who were sitting by the fire in their flat, and there was a crash somewhere off-stage. The husband said merrily, "Sounds like the bathroom ceiling falling in" and the wife went to look – just in case – and it was.'

'Fascinating. I must remember. Are you going to sleep, Rodney? If you are I'll finish your drink and get on with my book.'

'Of course I'm not going to sleep. What, and miss the wonderful feeling of being on holiday? The first day of the hols. "Peace, perfect peace, with loved ones far away", though the hymn-writer didn't quite mean it like that. Well, they will be far away by Monday.'

The Reverend Rodney Chelmarsh, vicar of St Crispin's, Abbotsbourne, Kent, was beginning his annual month of freedom from parish and parishioners, and – a rare respite – from his thirteen-year-old daughter Helena, crippled by a progressive disease. Helena's character had been warped by the early loss of her mother and by formative years in the care of a nurse-companion who was now in Broadmoor, for a murder of which she had been declared not guilty by reason of insanity.

The nurse's obsessive devotion to the child was echoed in Helena's demanding possessiveness towards her young father and her jealous hatred of the girl he loved and would have married. Doran Fairweather, antiques dealer of Eastgate, the near-by resort, and Rodney's neighbour in Abbotsbourne, had tried very hard for her own sake and Rodney's to face the prospect of life in the same house as Helena, but she knew too well that it would have destroyed her, and her relationship with Rodney. And so their mutual love remained unratified, even unconsummated; a clergyman might not live in what would still, so near the end of the permissive twentieth century, be called sin.

He watched her, relaxed and graceful as a sleeping cat in her hammock, willow-slim and long-legged, just as tall as a woman should be. 'Amo, amas, I love a lass,' recited Rodney to himself (he had an irresistible propensity for quotation, often maddening to others). 'As a cedar tall and slender, Sweet cowslip's grace is her nominative case, And she's of the feminine gender.' Soft brown hair and eyes that were neither green nor grey nor brown, but jewels compounded of all three; pale pearly skin just beginning to turn faintly gold with the sun. Her twenty-six years were hard to credit.

He wondered if, just for once, he should lift her from the hammock and lay her on the warm grass and kiss her as such a girl should be kissed on such a summer day. The garden of Bell House, Doran's home, was ringed with trees, invisible from the lane; no faces peered from the windows, for Doran lived alone since the departure of her housekeeper. He thought, on the whole, he would.

He was half-way out of his chair when the sharp click of the lattice gate arrested him. It was opening – they had visitors. Rodney said several unecclesiastical words to himself, and subsided.

'Company,' he told Doran, who made a face.

'Oh no! Who on earth . . . Howell. And Andrew. What have we ever done to deserve this?'

Howell Evans was Doran's partner in the small antique shop she owned in Eastgate, the seaside town some fifteen miles away. He was Welsh, slightly bent, more than slightly gay, a sharp dealer with large gaps in his knowledge but a wonderful head for figures. It was he who kept the business on its feet. His attitude towards Doran was a blend of criticism and grudging affection.

They advanced across the lawn, the short dark pit-pony of a Welshman and his boyfriend, the blond, almost colourless Andrew, who helped in the shop occasionally and roused very mixed feelings among the dealers who came to it. Doran, swinging her legs over the side of the hammock, viewed their approach without pleasure. She had been perfectly aware of Rodney's gaze and desires, which matched her own.

Once before Howell's sudden tactless arrival had spoiled their chance of what might have been a night spent together. Neither of them had forgotten that.

'I thought you were supposed to be in Wales?' was her uncordial greeting.

'Well we was,' Howell said. 'Did quite a bit of buying, didn't we. Plenty of old biddies up the north, foreigners you know, come there from Lancs and Yorks, don't know much, so we went knocking and pulled a fair bit of nice stuff.'

'You went round robbing old ladies: I see,' said Doran. 'Told them the usual story, I suppose – you'd pay them the earth for some worthless object, then picked out some nice things and got them thrown in for next to nothing.'

'What else? You don't complain when the goods come into stock, gal.'

'I suppose not. Anyway, what are you doing here?'

Howell's eyes were on the rustic table and the bottle of gin. 'I'm properly parched.' He licked his lips. 'Aren't you, Andrew? We been drivin' three hours without a stop. You got drinks out, I see. Wouldn't mind a drop, if you can spare it.'

'I'm sure there were plenty of places you could have stopped for tea. Oh well, sit down. There's a couple of chairs in the shed over there. You know Rodney Chelmarsh, don't you. Rodney, I don't think you've met Andrew Bynde.'

Rodney smiled politely in response to Howell's curt nod and Andrew's waved fingers, and prepared to pour drinks. 'I'll fetch some more glasses,' he said.

'Oh, would you? In the kitchen cupboard. And bring some tonic – *plenty* of tonic,' Doran added meaningly. 'Howell has a long way to drive.'

'That's all right,' Howell said airily. 'We take it in turns. Haven't you got no more proper chairs?' He eyed unfavourably the upright ones he had brought. 'Loungin' ones, like those?'

'No,' said Doran, who had. 'And you're not having Rodney's, so just settle down – those will do while you're here.' Which I trust won't be long, she added mentally. Howell was eying Rodney, who was coming towards them with a clutch of bottles and glasses, weighing up with a practised eye the spare slender figure, elegant height, and attractive features to which the dark-rimmed spectacles lent an intellectual air. One of these manly parsons the English went in for, thought Howell, who in his youth had been forced to attend a small and forbidding Bethesda administered by an equally small and forbidding Nonconformist preacher, pale from a life down the mines. This parson was too healthy-looking by half for a man of the cloth, not to mention half-naked in them shorts and sports shirt. Howell ventured a veiled reproach as Rodney set down the drinks.

'Proper tanned you are. Didn't find that in the pulpit, did you?'

'Well, no. I've got in quite a bit of tennis lately. Even the odd cricket match on a Sunday afternoon, with our second eleven. We've had a pretty good season, haven't we, Doran – three away wins and two home wins and a draw. No thanks to me, I'm an utter and absolute tail-ender.'

'That's not true, and you know it,' Doran said hotly. 'You know you . . . '

Howell jealously thought he detected a gleam of admiration in Andrew's eyes, as they dwelt on Rodney.

So, fancied butch types now, did he, even heteros. Well, it wouldn't do. Hastily he broke in.

'Reason we called on you, Doran, well, it's quite a story. Cheers, dears.' He gulped his gin. 'Thing is, we'd done Wales, filled the van, seen my old mam and a few of the boys, so we thought we'd head for the A5 and sort of down through the Midlands. North of Brum the roads got properly f . . . ' He glanced at Rodney. 'Properly fouled up with traffic, so we thought we'd branch off and sort of wander.'

'Why not?' Doran suppressed a sigh; it was going to be a long tale.

'Very pretty the country is, down there when you've got Brum behind you. Found some nice little pubs, didn't we, and let ourselves ease up for a change.'

11

'You must have needed a rest after all that knocking,' Doran said with a straight face.

'Yes, well. There wasn't much doing in the trade line, not in July, just tourists milling about and shops full of garbage, fakes, repro, *you* know. Then we . . . ' There was a fractional pause. 'We hit on a little place, nothing special but a good pub. Just happened we met a man one night, got talking, and he told us about this house.'

'What house?'

'Where this man lived, that had this clock. Well, you know me and clocks.' Doran did; he was a clock man, they were his passion. For a fine clock he would travel any distance and pay any price, within reason.

Andrew, looking for once faintly animated, broke in. 'Howell said –'

Howell shot him a darting glance, the equivalent of a kick on the ankle, and went on. 'I had to have it, Doran. He parted easy after I offered him a fair price. I brought it to show you – couldn't keep it to myself, and I didn't know if you'd be at the shop next week.'

'I shan't, I'm on holiday. All right, where is it?'

'In the van, locked up. Fetch it, Andrew.'

While Andrew was gone the three sat and looked at each other, lost for conversation. Doran was conscious of something strange, odd, hard to define, about the story she had just heard and the atmosphere Howell was exuding, as he busily lit a pungent American cigarette. In a few moments, she knew, it would be stubbed out, an offensive patch on the grass. Rodney was bored with Howell, disappointed that he no longer had Doran to himself, beginning to be apprehensive of the scene Helena might make when he went home, because it was almost their last evening before she left for the enforced holiday she resented having to take with her nurse. In the uncomfortable silence he said, 'Anybody know it's Lammas Day, the first of August? Known to the medievals as *Dies Mala,* because they thought it was unlucky. Also the Feast of Saints

Faith, Hope, Charity and their mother Wisdom, all martyrs.'

Howell laughed and coughed through smoke. 'So that's what happened to 'em – I always wondered.'

Doran said, 'Also the anniversary of Nelson's defeat of the French fleet off Aboukir, the Glorious First of August. It wasn't unlucky for *him*.'

'There's no answer to that.' It was a bad sign when Rodney subsided into television cliché. This pointless conversation was ended by the re-appearance of Andrew, bearing a large parcel which he put down on the grass, old brown paper with glimpses of newsprint beneath, firmly corded with tough string. Howell dropped on his knees beside it in a not inappropriate attitude of prayer, and began to cut the string with a clasp-knife of lethal appearance. Layer after layer of newspaper fell away, until at last they were looking at the core of the parcel. Howell was hardly breathing as he pulled away the last wrapping.

To Doran's eyes it was a superlative clock, and its price could only be guessed at, up among the tens of thousands of pounds. About thirty centimetres high, it was a bracket clock of brass, mellowly gleaming, its sheen dimmed by time and fortunately not heightened by modern cleaning. Its dome was softly rounded like that of St Paul's, set about on four sides by a decoration centred by the royal arms, a lion and unicorn holding between them a shield engraved C.R. Between the front baluster pillars was engraved *Edwardus East Fecit 1666.*

Doran joined Howell on the grass. As yet she hardly dared to touch the delicate finial on the dome, pepper-pot shaped, the flowers and leaves engraved within the dial, the little rounded feet. Silently Howell turned it round and showed the backplate, where more flowers grew and blew – roses, tiny thistles, wild convolvulus – and a small gardener with pail and hoe moved across the scene. Above him, Edwardus East had proudly, lovingly repeated his signature.

13

'It's a weight-driven alarm,' Howell breathed, and with a touch set off a silver-golden chime like a fairy carillon, a lovely turbulence which stopped with a protesting whirr after the stroke of one.

'Needs repairing,' Andrew volunteered. Howell was not listening, only searching Doran's face for a reaction which she was almost too stunned to express.

She sat back on her heels. 'I don't know what to say. What a wonderful, marvellous thing.' No point in asking if it were genuine; there are some antiques which cannot be faked any more than one could fake a living child. 'Where in heaven's name did you get it? And how much did you pay for it?'

Howell rose and went back to his chair, still intent on the clock. 'I told you, man in a little village. Getting rid of all his good stuff, wanted the money. And as for what I give him, it was out of my own bank. I'd never have drawn all that lot out of the kitty, Doran, you know that. I'll get it back, I've got a buyer lined up.'

'Oh – who?'

Without answering, he said, 'I've got to have it myself, first. Just for a bit, to get the feel of it. *You* know.'

'He's going to take it to bed with him,' put in Andrew, with a snort of mirth. 'Poor look-out for me.'

'Shut up. You do understand, don't you, Doran?'

Doran glanced at Rodney for some sage comment, but he was inwardly collecting bits of Keats and stringing them together, half-aloud. 'Buds and bells and stars without a name . . . '

'I understand that you wanted to show it to me, Howell. But not really how you came across such a rarity, just by accident. I mean, Tompions turn up, Knibbses turn up, but Edward Easts . . . I thought they were all in museums or America. And how could you possibly manage to pay for it, unless you've been keeping something from me and you're a closet millionaire? That I don't understand.'

14

Howell's mouth was sulky. 'Then I'm not going to say no more. I could've just taken it back to Eastgate, then you'd never have seen it, but I thought I'd give you the chance. Right. That's it.' He had begun to wrap the clock up, swathing its beauty in dirty crumpled newspaper, and Doran felt an irrational impulse to snatch it from him and carry it to her own drawing room, half a century more modern, yet a more right and gracious setting for such a treasure than Howell's tarty cottage or the prosaic shop. And the little rooms at the back of Bell House were Stuart, it would like them . . . But it was gone, wrapped, hidden, Cinderella back in rags.

'Thanks for the drink,' Howell was saying, apparently restored in temper. 'I'll give you a bell Monday, right? Don't worry about us and the shop, we'll manage.'

'I'm sure you will.' One way or another.

Howell gave her arm a brisk pat, like someone reassuring a nervous dog. 'And don't you worry about the price of the East, I'll get the top of the market for it and give you a nice profit, honest I will. Our books is lookin' pretty run down, you know, buckets of red and a rotten little bit of black, so you can't afford to turn your nose up, can you, like you done just now.' He added, hurriedly, 'Had to cut Vic Maidment in on it, more's the pity.'

When they were gone and the lattice gate was shut behind them Rodney said, 'Pardon my ignorance, but what was all that about? A beautiful clock, yes. Any more to it?'

'A lot. Not only beautiful, but extremely rare, by one of the greats, Edward East. His life covered most of the seventeenth century and he was clockmaker to Charles I and Charles II.'

'Hence the C.R.'

'Right. He lived to be ninety-something, so it must have been a healthy life. His work's very uncomplicated, usually – perfect proportions, but simple. That clock's very ornate for him, even a bit pretty-pretty, but

15

it could have been a commission from someone who liked them that way.'

'The royal ladies of pleasure? Busty Barbara, Pretty Witty Nell, Fubsy Portsmouth?'

'Very possibly. But there's no doubt that it *is* by East. What I'd like to know is where it's been all this time, and how the hell anyone like Howell could have afforded it. I just don't understand.'

'Could it be . . . would it be indelicate to suggest that all was not well with the transaction?'

'Oh, I know Howell's bent, I've caught him out several times, but only in quite minor things, and this is a very big one. His chum Victor Maidment's even benter, and a nasty bit of work. Howell just daren't have nicked anything as conspicuous as that, or bought it, knowing it was hot. We get lists of stolen property from the police all the time, and if that's on one of them he hasn't a remote chance of getting rid of it – and what's more, I should take the rap for it, as the shop-owner.'

'Perhaps a grateful customer gave it him, in return for services rendered.'

'I dread to think what services. No, anyone who gave that away would be certifiable. All right in Good King Charles's day, not now. So what's the answer?'

Rodney shook his head. 'I wish I knew, but you're the expert. And speaking of time, I've got to go now. I promised to have supper with Helena.'

'Oh dear.' Doran had hoped against hope that he would spend the evening with her. Not a natural cook, she had painstakingly taught herself how to make the prawn soufflé Rodney particularly liked, and beside the fresh prawns in the fridge sat materials for a pretty salad and a bowl of equally fresh fruit marinading in wine, to be served in two halves of melon, *très chic.* In what passed for her wine cellar lay a precious bottle of Pouligny Montrachet which somebody had brought her from France, waiting for its final chilling to perfection.

So much for optimism. Disappointment tinged her voice with bitterness as she said, 'Just as you like.'

'It isn't just as I like at all, and you know it. Do you think I don't want to stay, and do you also think I don't know what it would lead to, if I did? Sit down, I'm going to preach you a short sermon. If you imagine I get some kind of priggish enjoyment out of leading a life of celibacy and keeping you at arm's length, you're dead wrong. I don't. It makes me feel a worm, sometimes, apart from anything else. If I may mention Keats, and I promise I won't dwell on him, when his publisher asked him if he really meant anything so shocking in *The Eve of St Agnes* as Porphyro actually getting into bed with Madeline, he answered tartly that a man might consider himself a eunuch who would leave a maid in such a situation.'

'I have read the *Letters*, thank you. And I'm not a maid, in case you'd forgotten.'

'Don't interrupt. What I'm trying to say is that it's not a matter of principle. I just don't feel free to act as I want to, not only because of my job but because of my home situation. When that changes everything else will, I hope.'

'There's something in the law about consenting adults in private.'

Rodney got up from his chair. 'I'm going now, before either of us says anything we regret. I shan't see you tomorrow – Father Oliphant's taking the eight and the ten o'clock, and I'm going to lunch with them afterwards to put him in the picture about various things, not that he doesn't know the parish well.'

In the hall he stepped into the jeans he had draped on a chair. 'Just in case it might look bad to leave your house wearing shorts.'

At the front door, still fighting back the hurtful things she would have liked to say, Doran pointed to the dusking sky. 'There's a new moon.'

Rodney whipped off his spectacles. 'Then I mustn't

17

look at it through glass. Now.' He looked up at the thin silver sickle, glimmering like a young ghost in the still azure sky. 'I wish,' he said, and with a swift kiss on Doran's nose ran lightly down the path and shut the gate firmly behind him.

From a garden in the lane a cat appeared, jumped on a low wall and made for Rodney, mewing and purring alternately in pleasure as he stroked it with a professional touch. He would have liked a vicarage cat, but Helena had been jealous of the kitten a neighbour had given them, and he had found her tormenting it. This cat appeared to have notions of following him home.

'On such a night as this, Pussy,' he addressed it, 'Troilus, methinks, mounted the Trojan walls, and sighed his soul towards the Grecian tents, where Cressida lay that night. Be thankful you're not a tomcat, Pussy, as I see by your aspect you are not. Now go home to your loving family, and I shall go back to mine.'

His loving family, his stunted daughter Helena, put her thin deformed arms about his neck and held him tightly. 'You've got to spend every minute with me, Daddy, every minute of tonight and tomorrow because on Monday you're sending me away.'

'I'm not sending you away, darling. You're going for a splendid holiday with Arline.'

'I hate Arline.'

'No, you don't. And I shall be out quite a bit of tomorrow, seeing Father Oliphant – he's staying at the Rose with his family, before moving in here.'

'And I suppose *she'll* be there – at the Rose.'

'Mrs Oliphant? Of course.'

'No, I mean Her, that Doran, your tart.'

Arline Bray, Helena's nurse, advanced on her like a handsome battleship. Her New Zealand tones were as loud and formidable as the voice of the guns.

'Helena, one more dirty word like that out of your mouth and I'll stick a spoonful of mustard in it. I mean it, now, so you just belt up, will you?'

                              *   *   *

Doran, alone and no longer angry but deflated, fed her
visiting hedgehog and watched it trot away across the
lawn. At least it was happy, or so she hoped. The
house, when she went inside, was very quiet. Since the
departure of her housekeeper after last year's tragic
summer Doran had come to relish the freedom of
having her home to herself, and the cleaning and
shopping had been taken over by Vi Small, the village
Jill-of-all-trades, a fruitful source of cheerfulness and
gossip. Tonight, since Rodney was not with her, she
would escape into an old, calming, familiar book.

She chose *The Phoenix and the Carpet.* Inside the
wellworn cover was her baptismal name in her own
childish writing: Dora Ann Fairweather, Her Book, 1970,
12 Springhills Avenue, Oxford, Oxfordshire, England,
The World. Dora Ann was long forgotten, Doran lived.

She settled on the window-seat and began to read.
But the spell of E. Nesbit refused to work its usual
magic. Curiously, it was not Rodney's face that came
between Doran and the page, but the face of the clock.
The clock so mysteriously acquired, explained by such
a fishy tale. What provenance had it? What owner had
kept it hidden, and why – for fear that to advertise its
presence might attract burglars? How had Howell paid
for it, and who was the man in the pub who had so
casually mentioned it?

Of course she should never have let Howell go
without demanding a full explanation, since any
follow-up, such as an arrest, would involve her personally. Tomorrow she would drive down to Eastgate and
confront Howell (who could be relied on to sleep until
noon before moving on to the Port Arms for the first
drink of the day). Unless he could produce convincing
details she would forcibly remove the clock.

And do what with it – take it into protective custody,
report it to the police? She put down *The Phoenix and*

the Carpet and began to draw the clock on the margin of a magazine page: its outline, its charming dome, the flowers on the dial, the decorative backplate . . .

Edward East's signature had been on the backplate, as well as above the dial. And something else? But memory could not reconstruct any other inscription. In the centre of the backplate, between the escapement and the hour-wheel and the tiny gardener at the foot, was engraved a Tudor rose, much larger than the flowers bordering it . . . and a name.

Quite suddenly there came to Doran the absolute conviction that somewhere, some time, she had seen the clock before.

CHAPTER TWO

The Lady Jane was tall and slim,
The Lady Jane was fair . . .

As with so many dead certainties, Doran's belief that she would find Howell at home was mistaken. In the quiet of Sunday morning the only people she aroused with her performance on the dolphin-shaped knocker were the neighbours. A grey head looked out of an upstairs window of the cottage next door, and a rough voice urged her to desist, though in less polite terms.

A walk down the side alley and round the back of the cottage showed opened curtains up and down and no sign of life. Doran pressed her nose flat against a pane, in the faint hope of seeing the clock. Predictably, it was not visible. How easy it appeared when characters in television dramas found an unlocked window, flung a leg casually over the sill, ransacked the place and left by the same method. Doran knew that if she even located a vulnerable window the rest of the operation would go disastrously wrong, by the operation of Sod's Law.

At the shop she found the back room piled up with the loot brought from Wales, all still in wrappers apart from a box of small miscellaneous objects and a garden statue. It was hard not to speculate whether the owner of the garden had seen it go, but Doran reproved herself for scepticism; she was not, after all, in partnership with a known crook.

The garage where the van lived was locked. Doran

had forgotten to bring her key, but a glance through the cobwebby window into the interior gloom showed that the van was not there.

She drove to the Port Arms, and just after opening time presented herself at the bar. None of the regulars was yet in. They were, presumably, disentangling themselves from their sheets and a mound of Sunday newspapers.

'Seen Howell?' she asked George, the landlord, as he pushed her beer across. He shook his head.

'Didn't know he was back. Been home, hasn't he, to Welsh Wales?'

'That's right. He got back yesterday. You'll be seeing plenty of him for the next fortnight – I'm taking a bit of a holiday.'

'You do that, love. Hardly worth keeping open this time of year, is it?'

Doran took her tankard and a ploughman's lunch out to a bench in front of the pub, and sat contemplating the calm sea, where deep grey merged into Mediterranean blue, which in turn became indigo, the dark sapphire of Cornish waters, rare off this Channel coast. In the waves figures splashed and heads bobbed; an excited dog ran barking up and down the shingly shore. One or two little boats were out, and in the distance a tanker moved languidly across the horizon.

She wondered if she would really do what she had told George – take a holiday. She had mentioned it to one or two people, including Howell, without any clear idea of what she would do with it: only the unacknowledged consciousness that Rodney would be free.

In previous years, when Nancy had been in charge of Helena, he had gone away for a few days at a time, to look at cathedrals or walk in the Lake District. Once he had gone to Brittany, once to friends in Suffolk, once to a religious retreat, from which he had come back in a very bad temper. Doran wondered whether he had

22

always been alone. The query returned now, slyly clawing and biting. He would have a month of complete liberty, and he would certainly not spend it in Abbotsbourne. And judging by his mood the previous day it was probably just as well.

She waited after her lunch was finished, in case Victor Maidment, Howell's dealer friend, should appear. It was not for the pleasure of his company, since she had always thought him mean and spiteful and a twister, but he had been in on the acquisition of the clock and could be questioned. But he failed to materialize: he would. She drove to his flat and rang the bell: no answer. He lived alone as far as she knew.

She left a note at the cottage telling Howell to telephone her, and drove back to Abbotsbourne. The valley country was in its holiday mood under the placid sun, fields full of caravans, gardens where families lounged or splashed in pools, sheep and cows gathered under shady trees. On the edge of the village the first eleven was playing a half-day match, its star batsman, Bob Woods, at the wicket. Outside the pavilion reclined his pretty wife Barbary with their baby son Donald, thus christened in honour of Bradman. No child of Bob's would be allowed to grow up without a bat in its hand.

Doran remembered the shadows of the previous summer, when the cricket field itself was menaced by evil. The house where that embodied evil had lived was gone, bulldozed to make room for a small private estate of executive houses. Outside Laburnum Cottage in the High Street a young man was pushing a lawnmower up and down past a very new pram. Doran hoped that any traces of white magic left by Stella Meeson would be beneficial to the pram's occupant. Stella and Marcia Fawkes were gone, quiet refugees from old scandal. Abbotsbourne was looking up.

Back in her own garden Doran dragged out a folding table and covered it with encyclopedias of antiques,

23

books on clocks and clockmakers, old stock books kept in the cellar for reference, annual price guides – anything which might provide a clue to her elusive impression of a previous sight of the clock. No echoes woke. After two hours of eye-wearying work she was startled by a voice.

'Hi! Am I interrupting you?'

The voice came from the other side of the fence on the left of the garden. Magnolia House next door had recently been bought by a couple whom Doran had glimpsed occasionally, politely greeted, and thereafter forgotten, since a row of silver birches effectively screened off their garden and made neighbourliness unnecessary. Their name, according to Vi, was Berg. He was some sort of travelling salesman and she was a model, really quite glamorous for Abbotsbourne, was Vi's comment.

What Doran could see of Mrs Berg was certainly an improvement on the usual female villager. Blonde hair, expensively high-lighted and fashionably gelled and spiked, stood out round a face that had acquired its tan a long way from Kent. It wore no make-up beyond perfectly applied eye-liner and shadow.

'Not a bit,' Doran replied. 'I was just looking through . . . things.'

'Then come round and have some tea – time we got to know each other.'

Magnolia House was newer than Bell House, built in the sedate 1830s, stuccoed and painted a pristine ivory with woodwork of almond-green. Somebody had done a lot of work on the once-neglected garden, with the aid of a nursery and ready-grown plants, now blooming in profusion. Doran resolved to send her part-time gardner Ozzy round to see just how a flower border should look. A huge tulip tree, for which the house had been named, dominated the end of the half acre.

The Bergs were both tall, spare and elegant. Richenda Berg, as she introduced herself, was perhaps thirty-five. She had brown sensational legs ending, eventually, in a white one-piece swimsuit which displayed a figure at once svelte and voluptuous. Her long throat was set off by a necklace of primitive design but, Doran suspected, of real rubies and turquoises. She had the straight back and noble carriage of a dancer. She would, Doran felt, have knocked spots off Helen of Troy.

Cosmo Berg could have been her elder brother. His face was ruggedly handsome and his tan looked as though it had come from some highly romantic form of sailing before the mast. His fair moustache was a deeper gold than his hair, and his eyes were sailor-blue. Viking royals, King Olaf and Thyri the Fair.

Doran was by now feeling unhealthily pale, insignificant and not a day over fifteen. Richenda's bubbling cordiality soon made her forget herself.

'We thought it was high time we got to know you – living next door and hardly exchanged a word yet.'

'Yes, I'm sorry, I'm not at home much—'

'I know, you're in antiques, quite fascinating. You'll hate our house, it's full of cheap-but-cheerful things we've picked up all over the place in Cosmo's travels.' She was busy laying a low pine table with a very nice modern Doulton tea-service and plates of goodies. 'We decided we really had to settle down somewhere in England, in spite of everything, strikes and the weather and no servants and all that.'

'With all its faults you love it still,' said Doran helpfully, before realizing that sententious bits of Cowper were not likely to mean much to Richenda, who was pouring tea and chattering merrily. Not much of the chatter was directed at her husband, Doran noticed. She was conscious of his speedwell eyes on her constantly. Was it imaginable that with a wife who might quite possibly have been Miss World in her time Cosmo Berg could be impressed with her own understated, pastel English looks?

It was. Instinct would have told her as much, even if one large bronzed hand had not enclosed and held hers during the innocent process of handing her a cup of tea. Over the rim of it she stole surreptitious glances at him. He was older than he had seemed at first, perhaps not far off fifty, now that the sun was full on his face etching deeper the lines on it. Curious, how a moustache suited some men and made others look like members of a barber-shop ensemble. She wondered how it would feel to be kissed by a man with a moustache; details of the last occasion had faded from her memory, though it had certainly involved a swarthy student wearing a CND badge and a gilt medallion tangling with the mat of hair on his chest. How unselective one had been then . . .

The moustache curved upwards above a smile that seemed to reflect her thoughts. She blushed furiously.

'. . . nice working in Eastgate,' Richenda was saying. 'Tell you what, I'll come in with you one morning and do some shop-hounding and afterwards we'll have lunch. I know a little place on the cliff road, not terribly posh but he's half-Greek half-French and does his own cooking, quite amusing on a good day. What about that?'

'Lovely,' Doran said, not meaning it. Cosmo asked her some questions about the Trade and she perceived a sharp intelligence behind the golden looks. He was, it proved, not a travelling salesman but a representative of a prestigious marketing firm based in London. Buying and selling interested him, clearly.

'Is it true,' he asked, 'that you dealers don't want the public in your shops, and if so, why?'

'Well. Yes and no. They're not where the money comes from, unless they're collectors or want something enough to pay our price for a good piece. Actually, I don't mind them, I quite like selling bits, especially when I know something's going to a good

26

home. But they can waste one's time, and sometimes they break things – you often see a notice hung up, "Lovely to look at, delightful to hold, But if you break me consider me sold." It doesn't stop them, though.'

' "Lovely to look at, delightful to hold." ' Cosmo repeated the words with his eyes on hers, then moving down to her mouth, and up again. Doran felt the blush surging back. There was something in the old Astaire song about 'Heaven to kiss'. He remembered that too, of course. She thought she saw a flashing glance pass between husband and wife.

Richenda said, 'When I was changing for dinner last night I saw a really fetching man coming away from your house. In fact I stopped and stared – I hope he didn't see me and think me rude.'

Doran was annoyed. She did not in the least want to chat about Rodney to Richenda, or to anybody, with the smart of rejection still alive. 'Oh? I don't know who that would have been.'

'Tall, nice tan, clever face. Glasses. A bit like Dustin Hoffman in *The Graduate.*'

'I'd hardly describe Dustin Hoffman as tall,' observed Cosmo.

'Oh, well, have it your own way. Perhaps I mean Michael Caine. Only darker.'

'Ah.' Doran's tone was throw-away. 'That would be Rodney Chelmarsh, our vicar.'

'Vicar! You're joking. He's too young, anyway.'

'Not at all. He's thirty-nine, just.'

'How incredible. Married, I suppose?'

'No, a widower.' Doran was determined not to blush again but found it hard not to snap. She pretended to catch sight of her watch, exclaimed at the time, thanked Richenda for a delightful tea and said that they must come for drinks as soon as she got back from her holiday.

'Going away somewhere lovely?'

'I haven't decided. I'll probably point the car

27

westwards and finish up in Cornwall. The sea at East-gate this morning made me think of St-Anthony-in-Roseland.'

Richenda smiled, a sunburst smile revealing a Hollywood galaxy of perfect teeth. 'You're a real romantic, I can see that.'

'So they tell me. Well, goodbye, and thank you again.'

Cosmo Berg saw her to the gate, one hand beneath her elbow, gently steering and at the same time conveying a perfectly clear message. She was surprised to find the contact quite pleasant; indeed very pleasant. His parting from her was a model of friendliness with something much warmer behind it. He was, she decided, a most interesting neighbour.

At home she shut up all the books and carried them in. They told her nothing, and her mood was changed. She washed her hair, took a long, soothing bath scented with wickedly expensive oil, and changed into the kingfisher blue caftan which was her favourite garment, before settling down to watch a restful, escapist TV serial.

When it had finished she telephoned Howell's number. There was no answer. The clock's image floated in her subconscious, tried against various backgrounds, a museum showcase, a domestic mantelpiece, a colour photograph (but would that have illustrated the backplate as well?) None of them fitted. The unravelling of its mystery would have to wait.

Rodney stood beside Arline Bray's car watching her load the last of the luggage into the boot. He did not offer to help. To Arline's steely strength a heavy suitcase was what a matchbox would be to a lesser person. Tall, whipcord tough, with the broad shoulders and slight hips of a lightweight boxer, Arline was as a-sexual as an exercise bicycle: her presence at the vicarage as

Helena Chelmarsh's nurse caused no gossip, even among the most active mischief-makers of Abbotsbourne. She had a rocking-horse face, a high colour and large strong teeth, both no doubt the end product of a healthfood diet which yet included meat whenever she could get it. Alcohol she regarded as poison but drank quantities of undoctored fruit juice. She was very expensive to keep.

In spite of that, Rodney was fervently grateful for her astringent care, which had improved Helena's health and general well-being. Arline was contemptuous of the 'soft' treatment Helena was receiving. She neither liked nor disliked the child, but believed strongly in not indulging whims, tantrums, fancies and crazy ideas. If Helena became thwarted enough to give way to hysterics she was taken smartly to her room and locked in, her shrieks ignored. The treatment worked, unless Rodney tried it on his own.

For him Arline had tolerance mixed with contempt. The only men she counted as men were the sort of rough types who had pioneered her native country and Australia, if they had ever existed except in her mind, which Rodney sometimes wondered. He guessed that she had little respect for men, or perhaps for anyone but herself. She looked on religion as a load of superstitious nonsense, only bothering to converse on it with him when she thought he could be provoked into answering back. He was too controlled to rise to this, and needed her help too much.

'Right,' Arline declared. 'All in, let's go. If that kid's bellyaching again tell her to shut up.'

'I think she just wanted to ask if her special cushion was packed,' Rodney offered.

'It is, far as I know. If not, she'll hev to make do, won't she. C'mon, time we went.' Rodney was shoved unceremoniously out of the way as she hauled her long muscular legs into the driving seat and gave the engine a raucous start. 'Send y' a postcard whin we git there.'

'Please do. And have a lovely time.' Rodney's last sight was of Helena's tear-streaked face and the back of Arline's head, straight, uncompromisingly set towards Devon, on whose coast they were booked into a seaside residential hotel with special facilities for invalid care. Helena would be looked after round the clock, or as far round it as necessary, while Arline walked, jogged, played squash with anyone brave enough to take her on, or, weather permitting, revelled in wind-surfing. It was an expensive treat, but Rodney grudged not a penny of it. The change was certain to do Helena good, keep Arline in temper and put her off thoughts of moving on. She had been travelling since finishing her nursing course in her late teens; he dreaded the day she would announce that she was ready to set out on the trail again.

And it would give him the break he so much needed from the tension of living with Helena. He refused to put her in an institution; Arline was the answer to home care for his beloved, dreadful daughter.

He telephoned Doran and got no reply. The vicarage was no longer his. Father Sydney Oliphant and his large family were all over it, and he was relegated to a small austere attic room where he would be in nobody's way. The parish was happy with Father Oliphant who was officially retired on private money but often dropped in as guest preacher. The Oliphants, mother Kate and the teenage brood, loved the Victorian house and its big rambling garden – they were happy too, and their West Highland White terrier was having the time of its life chasing imaginary rats and rabbits. It romped up to Rodney as he lay on the grass with *Martin Chuzzlewit* in a secluded corner of the old orchard, among early unripe windfalls. He caressed its head and watched it go barking on its way, envying its youth and carefree manner of life. His mind was a confusion of intense relief at Helena's absence, guilt at feeling such relief, and a heavy, flat lethargy of anti-climax. He was free, and did not know what to do with his freedom. After an hour or so he wandered into the church and sat there alone.

Indoors, he telephoned Doran again. This time she answered. There was a touch of chill in her tone.

'It's me,' he said unnecessarily. 'They've . . . ' It would have sounded too much like rejoicing to say, 'They've gone.' He altered it to 'Can I come over? I'd ask you, only the Oliphants are sort of rampant . . . '

There was a silence. 'I wasn't really expecting company, I've just got back from Eastgate and I'm rather tired.'

'Oh. I'm sorry. I'll go along to the courts and see if anyone's free for a game.'

'Do that.'

Rodney sighed. 'Well, that settles where I sleep tonight.'

'I *beg* your pardon?'

'Don't mention it. The Oliphants have a nice terrier. I'll go and join him. In the dog-house, in case I haven't made myself clear.'

He was relieved to hear Doran laugh. 'I see. Yes, I was a bit sharp, but I've had a frustrating two days, and somehow I thought you'd be busy, tidying up and that sort of thing.'

'I was, until this afternoon, rushing about making straight in the desert an highway for the Oliphants. I never stopped until lunch – panting Time toiled after me in vain.'

A pause. 'What did you say?'

'Which bit?' asked Rodney, surprised.

'Just the last. It was "panting Time toiled after me in vain", wasn't it? Where does that come from?'

'I really can't recall – something someone wrote about Shakespeare. Probably Johnson – it usually *is* Johnson.'

At the other end of the line Doran made a curious

noise, between a gasp and a crow. 'That's it! Can you come over now, quick? Very important!'

Almost at Bell House, Rodney's swift steps were halted by a voice.

'Good afternoon. It *is* the vicar, isn't it?'

Richenda Berg, in a clinging couture sun-dress of shimmering black, was smiling radiantly, secateurs in hand. She had intended to be nursing a cluster of roses, but he had appeared before she could gather them. Doran's telephone was near the French window, sound carried on a still day, and Richenda was an expert at putting two and two together.

Rodney was tempted to reply with the tag-line of an old chestnut, 'Madam, I *am* the vicar,' but contented himself with, 'That's right. Hello.'

'Hello. I'm Richenda Berg – we haven't been here very long, but my next-door neighbour told me who you were, and I thought I'd introduce myself. What a gorgeous day, isn't it?'

'Lovely. I hope I'll be seeing you in church – and your husband. Just now I'm on holiday, but I'm sure you'd like my locum tenens.' He was not sure of anything of the kind, and quite sure that this dazzling creature was not of the stuff from which devout congregations were made. 'Nice to meet you – excuse me, I must rush,' he added, leaving her gazing after him with the smallest shadow of a frown on her honey-skinned brow.

Doran opened the door before he had knocked at it. 'Come in. I've got something to tell you. Let's stay in, *she's* in their garden and I'm sure she'd listen.'

'If you mean your neighbour the Blonde Bombshell, she was at the front just now. And what have you been telling her about me?'

'Nothing, only who you were. She saw you on Saturday and asked. I know she's a perfect Venus and

32

I'm sure you're fascinated, but this is much more important. Sit down.'

'Venus fly-trap, I should say. It eats everything alive that settles on it . . . All right, I'm listening.'

'Well, what you said, about panting Time, suddenly clicked with me. I remembered what I've been trying and trying to remember – where I'd seen that clock before. Somebody said that line then, because the clock had a connection with Shakespeare – it was an erudite-looking man at the back of the room.'

'What room?'

'I'm just going to tell you. It was a room in an old manor-house, somewhere near Stratford-on-Avon, and I went there while I was up at Oxford. I'd been before, from school.' She did not add that she had gone with her first lover, Ian, whose abandonment of her had devastated her life for a time: perhaps it was her reluctance to think of him that had blocked her memory until now. 'It was a funny, shabby old house, very ancient and historic but shockingly neglected, and the old lady who owned it was the widow of a famous artist, Timberlake, one of the Camden Town School. He ran off with a model and it sent his wife off the trolley. She went into an asylum for a year or so, then came back to the manor house and ran it as a show-place. Are you listening?'

'I'm all ears. Pray continue your narrative.'

'The place was full of rubbishy paintings that she said were by her husband, but I knew they weren't; she'd probably done them herself. She was obsessed with him, terribly sad. But there were a lot of good things as well, not only pictures but furniture in an awful state of dirt and disrepair. One of them was Howell's clock.'

'Go on.'

'Try to stop me . . . Old Lady T. didn't know much about it, and I didn't myself at the time, not being into antiques then, but she did point out one thing. Do you remember the Tudor rose engraved in the middle of the backplate? Well, there was an inscription round it, in very tiny script, and it said *Rose Hathaway*.'

'The Bard's wife's family.'

'The same. Rose was a daughter of Thomas Hathaway, an in-law of Shakespeare's daughter Susanna, who married twice and left a complicated will. I haven't looked it up yet but I'm going to. But I have looked in a museums guide. Honeyford House is still open and Lady Timberlake's still alive. It's not National Trust, just her own property.'

Rodney pondered. 'Does that suggest to you the sort of things that it does to me?'

'I shouldn't wonder. I've spent all day on it. I went to Eastgate yesterday and first thing this morning. There was no sign that Howell had been at the shop, and he wasn't at the cottage. Andrew was, but I couldn't get anything out of him, except that Howell had gone off somewhere. That boy can be extraordinarily balky sometimes, though he does look so wet. Vic Maidment was out, too, just a Closed sign on the shop door.'

'Aren't there others you could ask?'

'There are. I've telephoned everyone I could think of, including a man in Berwick-on-Tweed. He didn't know anything about an East clock, and a lot of the others didn't answer. Ever tried getting hold of dealers in August?'

'No. So what are you going to do?'

'Go to Warwickshire and find out for myself if the clock's there still.'

'Couldn't you just telephone the house, whatsitsname, and save yourself the trouble?'

Doran regarded him pityingly. 'I did think of that. Nobody answered, and if they had I wouldn't guarantee Lady Timberlake to make sense at the other end. She was pretty far gone when I was there last – and I bet she's completely bananas by now. Stark mad in white satin.'

A silence fell. Doran had been half-hoping that her

announcement would draw a statement from Rodney about his own plans, but he stared out at the garden, watching birds drinking from a marble bowl.

'What are you thinking about?' she asked.

'Oh – just wondering what would have happened if I'd quoted something else, not that particular line. I could have said "The clock upbraids me with the waste of time" or "Time hath, my lord, a wallet at his back", or the bit from *Caesar* that's completely anachronistic but fits in perfectly well... all connections between Time and Shakespeare, but would they have done the trick?'

'I've no idea.' Doran wondered why she felt faintly cross. 'Well, never mind that, how did the departure go this morning?'

'All right. Arline gave her usual impersonation of an armoured tank and Helena seemed fairly resigned until the actual moment. She'll enjoy it when she gets there, of course. Abbotsbourne's pretty boring for her, especially when Susan Lockett's away during the school hols, and she gets no lessons. I've said I'll go down and see her when they've settled in.'

'Of course you must. Stay for supper?'

'Don't think I will, if you don't mind. Kate very kindly asked me to share with them – I can't think why, it must be a drag for them to have the incumbent still on the premises, but I know she's made a pie, and Arline's pies are atrocious.'

'Then you mustn't miss it, must you?' Doran said brightly.

As Rodney strolled, deep in thought, past the hedge of Magnolia House, Richenda bobbed up from behind it.

'Hello again! Goodness, we must stop meeting like this. How beautifully cool you look, but it's still steamheat, isn't it. Why don't you come in for a drink?' She gave a sly kick aside to the magazine she had been reading on the lawn as she waited for him.

Rodney was torn between an extreme reluctance to say Yes and an extreme disinclination to say No.

'Well its very kind of you. Just for two minutes, then.'

The expensively furnished drawing-room was empty but for himself and Richenda, offering him an array of bottles. 'Your husband isn't home yet?'

'My husband's in Berlin,' said Richenda. 'Scotch, gin, vodka, Kir, tequila, Pernod? Have whatever you like.' She moved a bottle strategically to afford him a view of a cabinet photograph behind it, a study of herself wearing a mysterious smile, an assortment of studio shadows, and nothing else.

CHAPTER THREE

. . . If she slept in any bed,
It was not in her own

Vi Small silenced the strident morning voice of the vacuum cleaner and substituted her own as Doran appeared in the hall, carrying a cardboard box.

'I see you got the car out – thought you wasn't going to be working this week.'

'I'm not. I'm going away, today if I'm ready in time. I wanted to get some of the rubbish out of it – then perhaps you could take that roaring thing over the upholstery.'

'Righto. Not like you to be taking holidays, is it? Well, a change is as good as a feast, that's what I always say. Bit of a change for me, working at the vicarage, with them Oliphants all over the place, like a swarm of bees, coffee-cups everywhere and seven beds to make. Father Oliphant they call him, and they're dead right – did you know they've got a married daughter in Norwich as well? Talk about rabbits.'

'Yes. But . . .'

'Still, at least they're civil – "please would you mind" and "thank you very much" not like that Arline – our Bossy Aussie, I call her, might as well have a kangaroo jumping down your throat.'

Doran no longer bothered to point out that Arline came from New Zealand; in Vi's mind it was indistinguishable from its neighbour. Vi rattled on.

''Spect the vicar's glad to be shut of her, even if he's got to live in that poky little attic and share the

37

bathroom with all that lot. Ruthie, that's the sixteen-year-old, she makes up in there, takes hours over it, and David uses enough hot water to swim in – I told him that when he runs the bath my hot tap in the kitchen goes off.' She embarked on a lengthy run-down of the appearances, characters and probable futures of the Oliphant family, while Doran, transferring miscellaneous debris from the box to the waste-paper basket, reflected on the loss it would be to Abbots-bourne culture if Vi only worked for one or two families and not for as many as she could cram into her packed week. Nobody would know anything about anybody else, whereas at present they knew everything. But at least it was a comfort that Vi was not malicious, and Doran had a feeling that she didn't spread the gossip about herself and Rodney.

'. . . old Mrs Pyecraft,' Vi was saying. 'Getting worse every day, she is, back to the days of Good Queen Victoria, and it's all real to her, realer than last Tuesday. "Vi," she says to me the other day, "Vi, what was me 'usband's name before we was married?" "Pyecraft," I says. "No, I mean his proper name, his Christian name?" "Fred," I says. "It was always Fred, dear." "Fred," she says, trying it over. "Fred, of course it was." Poor old soul.'

'You don't by any chance work for the people next door, at Magnolia House?' Doran asked.

'Me? Bless you, they don't need me. They got an agency cleaner from Eastgate, three times a week, comes on a motorbike, the full leather gear, helmet and all. Mean to say you've not noticed her? *He*'s abroad half the time and *she* lives the life of a lady, up to London when she wants a change, I suppose, but mostly lying about getting herself brown.'

'How do you know? I'm only next door, and I can't see their lawn through all those trees.'

'Well, the off-licence man caught her one day, when he took the stuff round the back, and it give him quite a turn . . .'

Clearing out the car gave Doran an appetite for doing the same thing with her wardrobe. She was amazed to find how many unfashionable, unbecoming and boring garments she had. Ozzy, who was half-gypsy, would do well at the Saturday market from the growing pile of jeans, shirts, and summer dresses on the floor, and what was left was not all that inspiring. But it would do for driving, and for whatever investigations, probably unsavoury, she would be making in Warwickshire.

As she hovered over a once-pretty Indian shirt printed with tropical fish, faded now but comfortable, the telephone rang. A familiar voice said, 'It's me.'

'Oh, good. You've just caught me. Another half-hour and I'd have been off.'

'Ah. In that case, will you look in here first? I mean before you're ready to leave.'

'Why can't you come round to me? I'm very busy packing.' Her voice was sharp with reluctance to leave him, with the briskness voices have on the departure platforms of railway stations.

'I can't explain – it would be . . . awkward. Too close to the cockatrice's den.'

'What on earth are you talking about, Rodney? Do make sense, I must get off by lunchtime.'

'Look, I've said I can't explain. Do please just slip round – I want to talk to you, and it's important. Doran, please.'

'Oh, all right, since you sound so solemn. What do I do, in the reign of the Oliphants – knock three times and ask for Rodney?'

'No, don't. I'll be in the little orchard – you can get in by the field gate.'

'Goodness, how romantic. I'll meet thee, Pyramus, at Ninny's tomb.'

For once he did not quip back.

Beside him on the dry grass under the gnarled apple

tree, Doran said calmly, 'You're going to tell me something dreadful, so get it over with. You've decided the situation's intolerable, or untenable or something, and you're going to put a stop to it. You're telling me now so that I'll have time to get used to the idea while I'm away. That's it, isn't it?'

Rodney sat up straight, staring. 'Is that what you've deduced from what I said the other night?'

'I suppose so.' To her dismay she felt her lower lip trembling.

'Well, allow me to break the news that you're dead wrong. Not so, but far otherwise. I'm going to tell you that I'm coming with you to Warwickshire.'

It was Doran's turn to stare. 'You're . . . what did you say?'

'You heard. Yes, I have decided something, upstairs in my little rookery and out here watching apples dropping off trees and wasps very slowly eating them. I've decided it's time I grew up. I'm a man, really very much like other men if you discount my angelic appearance, and I'm going to live like one, as far as possible without scandalizing people. As of Friday night I've been off duty at Crispin's, to all intents and purposes a layman. I've done the best I can for my family, for this month anyway. Nobody in Abbotsbourne gives a damn what I do on my holidays. Papa Oliphant's much more the beloved-pastor type than I am, and if they want to get buried or married or christened during August they'll thoroughly enjoy his ministrations. And, my dearest Doran, I've not been playing you fair. I'm going to put that right.'

'Are you . . . quite sure? I mean . . . conscience and that?'

'I've handed my conscience over to God,' Rodney said seriously. 'He'll do what He thinks proper. Somehow I don't think He'll grudge me a little happiness – after the last years. I'm trying not to

40

sound pi. Well? Aren't you going to say something?'

Doran put her arms round his neck and kissed him long and ardently.

'Yes, and yes, and yes. It's what I've wanted most, and I can't believe it. But you did say it, didn't you – you're coming with me?'

'Do you know, my darling, you went a very funny colour while all that was going on, a sort of delicate pale green with your freckles standing out like tiny copper coins. But now you've turned a lovely pink. Listen carefully. I've worked the whole thing out. How long will it take you to get ready?'

'Half an hour, unless I go mad with joy in the meantime, in which case I'll be found somewhere between here and there plaiting grass into my hair and singing about larks and clerks, like Mad Margaret.'

'I'd stick to Rose Maybud, if I were you – a change of baby-linen and a book of etiquette. There, now you've gone yet another shade of pink. Be serious. When you're ready, drive up Elvesham Avenue to Downs Corner, take the left fork, and park by St Eanswythe's. In a few moments, or even less, you'll see me thumbing a lift, with my little bundle of worldly goods tied up in a spotted handkerchief.'

'And your faithful cat?'

'Only if one follows me from the Downs Service Station, because I'm leaving my car in their garage – I've phoned them already and there's plenty of room. So we shall leave in one car, yours, and with luck nobody will inquire about mine. The Oliphants think I'm going off cathedraling. I didn't exactly say so but I sort of conveyed it. Right?'

The operation worked smoothly. As they drove from the green in front of the little, disused Saxon church Doran asked, 'Who was St Eanswythe?'

'Something to do with Ethelred the Unready – or

41

was it Ethelbert? Anyway, she renounced worldly pleasures in favour of a holy life.'

'Misguided girl,' said Doran. 'I take it we head for the motorway?'

Over their lunch of egg, bacon and chips at a wayside café near the M25 she asked him, 'What was all that about it being awkward, coming round to see me, and the cockatrice's den?'

Rodney finished the last of his coffee and beckoned a waitress to bring another cup. 'I've been wondering how to put it. For cockatrice, read Venus fly-trap. The lady we were discussing last night. She waylaid me going home.'

Doran let a beat of seconds go by. 'And?'

'She was very persuasive. Hospitable to a degree. I was offered a variety of exotic drinks. I decided to settle for a lager and said I had to get back to sup with the Oliphants. I got the impression that she wouldn't give up easily – in fact that she'd be very artistically on the lookout today. Local Siren gets Vicar Intoxicated. Her husband's abroad. I gather she's a very bored lady.'

'I see.' Doran saw perfectly well, without being told, that Rodney had been offered other things besides drinks. What she did not know, and he did not tell her, was that the conflict in his feelings had led, in an almost sleepless night, to the decision he had made. After all his care to avoid scandal involving Doran, he had found himself on the edge of succumbing to the invitation of a very beautiful and alluring woman, who would have ruined his reputation in return for brief excitement and another conquest. At that moment he was saved by a timely recollection of the *Ingoldsby* legend of the abbot who so unwisely dined with the Fiend disguised as a fair woman, and was rescued by St Nicholas. He would have enjoyed relating this thought to Doran, with its accompanying, unavoidable quote –

how the saint was hobnobbing away with a devil from hell, and how o'er a pint and a quarter of holy water he made the sacred sign, and dashed the whole on the soi-disant daughter of Old Plantagenet's line. Lager would hardly have had the same effect, even the brand which purports to get to the parts other beers cannot reach. Rodney had been obliged to substitute self-control. He had been late for the Oliphants' supper, but better late than never.

They were in Oxford by mid-afternoon, having tea at the Randolph. Afterwards Rodney insisted on a stroll round the town to look at colleges. He had been to Durham himself, but took pleasure in seeing Doran's educational haunts. She observed that St Hugh's was not especially a thing of beauty, having been built in 1886.

Rodney considered it. 'No. But you went there, which lends it lustre. Were you a rebellious girl, always getting locked out and having to sneak in through pantry windows?'

'On the contrary. Having been brought up in Oxford I found it held no delightful temptations for me.' Only one; she was disinclined to linger at Christchurch, Ian's college, though Rodney said that Dodgson had been mathematical lecturer there and that there were his fireplace tiles still to be seen, one showing a distinct likeness of the Snark.

Doran smiled and took his arm. What, after all, were old sorrows now? 'All right. We'll hang about in Tom Quad and you can recite as many bits of *Alice* as you like.'

'How very kind. No, I don't feel particularly Aliceish. We could go and hang about Balliol instead, so that I could recite Calverley. And Brasenose, because Barham was a Gentleman Commoner there – I could do you some very choice *Ingoldsby*.'

'Why do you keep on about Barham? That's the third time you've mentioned him this afternoon.'

'Purely Freudian. I'll tell you later. Time we got back to the car. Shall I take over the driving, unless you've got a one-driver-only clause in your insurance?'

'I haven't. Howell drives sometimes on a long buying trip, and he's quite good, when he's sober.'

The M40 was behind them, the A34 to Stratford ahead. At Chipping Norton they branched off left towards Stow-on-the-Wold, in Cotswold country, on a road that crossed rivers with the loveliest of names, Evenlode and Windrush; a country of hills that in the late summer afternoon had a mysterious haze of blue over their greenness, of honey-gold houses and half-timbered magpie cottages of immaculate charm. Gloucestershire, the county of Shallow and Silence.

Doran began to feel a rare excitement, an exhilaration that grew as their adventure became real to her. It was a mistake to say aloud that one was happy, had never been happier, because the spell might break, the iridescent bubble vanish into air. Rodney's face was impassive; a good driver, he watched the road and talked little.

They slowed down at every inn or hotel, studied it, and commented. 'Too new. Too big and pompous. Too flash, they wouldn't let us in looking like this.'

Outside a hamlet which had begun to climb a hill, then grown tired and given up, there was a rambling house of pale grey-gold Cotswold stone, its front smothered in pink roses. Through the side garden, among mushroom-topped staddling stones, ran a little stream which seemed to disappear under an arch in the wall. The inn-sign showed a trout rising among silver bubbles. They looked at each other, and Rodney stopped the car.

'This is it,' he said.

'If they're not full.'

'Go and see.'

44

'One thing. Who are we to be? I refuse to be contemporary and brazen and sign a different surname from yours. Look.' She displayed her left hand, on the third finger of which was a plain gold ring.

'Good heavens. I hadn't thought of that. I never noticed. Where did you get it?'

'It was Mother's.'

'Good, I'm glad it isn't out of your stock.'

' "All on this tray 10p"? Not likely. Just tell me what our name is.'

'I thought,' Rodney said diffidently, 'of Mr and Mrs R.H. Barham. Address, Tappington Everard, Kent. Don't laugh like that, it sounds flippant, for a respectable married woman. We'll be something else if you like – I just felt it was somehow apt.'

'It is, it is. I confess myself very partial to clergymen, even dead ones.' She went on purposefully towards the Leaping Trout, murmuring 'Mrs Barham, Mrs Barham, Mrs Barham.'

Rodney wondered if he had been over-presumptuous in taking the name of Richard Harris Barham, that excellent clergyman who had enriched literature by his *Ingoldsby Legends,* genial romps in sparkling verse through antique stories of his native Kent, with a proliferation of ghosts, naughty nuns, pompous priors, strong-minded saints and extraordinary incidents. A jolly man, Mr Barham, abounding, said his solemn biographer son, 'in goodwill towards men, and imbued with a spirit of active, though unostentatious piety.'

Surely such a man would not have tut-tutted at one of his brother clergy embarking on a romantic adventure with his beloved lady. True, he had died in 1845, by which time a spirit of distinctly ostentatious piety was beginning to spread in England. But surely his shade would grant a merry wink to his twentieth-century colleague, in the circumstances. Among all those farragos of cheerful nonsense he had left a song.

Oh, sweet is the breath of morn, when the sun's
first beams appear
Oh, sweet is the shepherd's strain, when it dies
on the listening ear;
And sweet the soft voice that speaks the wanderer's
welcome home –
But sweeter far,
By yon pale star,
With our true love thus to roam,
My dear!
With our own true love to roam.

Yes, Mr Barham, it is, agreed Rodney; and please
look kindly on us, if you're still about.

The inn could offer them a double room, at the back of
the house, facing up the hill. It was beamed and low
ceilinged, with a large divan-bed covered with a counter-
pane of flower-sprinkled blue. Rodney put down on it
the shoulder-pack which held all the luggage he had
brought.

'Which side will you have?'

'The middle,' Doran said,

There was no dining room, only a deep alcove
adjoining the bar. They ate something including
prawns, something including chicken, mushrooms,
cream and wine, and a fluffy syllabub because Rodney
said Shakespeare was fond of it, though he could
produce no evidence to that effect. Their drink was
local rough cider. The floor beneath their feet was
flagged, and the little stream had joined them indoors,
flowing through the bar between firm flagstone banks.
Rodney spoke little. Once he took her hand across the
table and held it. She saw that his own was shaking.

The bedroom window looked to the west, where
the sun was setting in a sky of Turneresque flame and
molten gold. They left the curtains undrawn.

In bed they found each other dear and familiar, strange, new and mysterious and beautiful beyond either's imagination. The whole of love-literature might have been on Rodney's lips, but it was no longer the time for other men's words. Against her shoulder, on her breasts, he said over and again, 'Doran, Doran.' And other things which none but they would ever know.

The sunset fires died into dusk, and dusk turned to dark. In a deep stillness they could hear only the babbling of the little stream as it meandered on its way from Evenlode. Then a church clock nearby broke the silence with twelve solemn strokes. Almost himself again, Rodney sat up and looked down at the glimmer of her face against the pillow. ' "We have heard the chimes at midnight, Master Shallow." '

'I never thought,' said Doran, 'to be addressed as Master Shallow on my bridal night. But there, life is full of surprises. At least it wasn't Jane Nightwork . . . '

The Trout's garden spread graciously all round the old house. Rodney and Doran had it to themselves after breakfast. An American party had paid their bill and left in a hired car; a grim-aspected elderly pair, with Retired Teacher written all over them, had gone tramping over the hills, armed with walking-sticks like knobkerries. The other visitors had melted away, unnoticed by the couple known as Mr and Mrs Barham, though they themselves had been noticed by staff and guests with amusement, envy and sentimental speculation. Their absorption in each other declared them honeymooners.

'Can't take her eyes off him,' reported the waitress to the female chef. 'They sat on the same side of the table, on that bench with the back to it, with hardly an inch between them.'

'It's a love-seat,' said the chef with a giggle. 'There's

47

one at Anne Hathaway's Cottage, that they reckon Shakespeare courted her on.'

'Bit hard, it must have been.' Both went off into giggles which reached the dining alcove where the supposed honeymooners were making a hearty breakfast.

'Isn't it a mercy that the appetites sort of go together,' observed Doran, finishing her fourth piece of toast. 'I don't think music's the food of love at all, whatever whatshisname may have said. Food is, if you ask me.'

'Bread of Heaven, bread of Heaven, feed me till I can no more . . .' Rodney's resonant baritone increased the level of giggles from the kitchen.

The garden patio was already warm in the morning sun. Almost on the border of the garden sheep grazed. 'Now those,' Rodney said, 'aren't anything like our sheep round Abbotsbourne. Much whiter, for one thing – more graceful, nicer figures.'

'They've been shorn,' Doran pointed out. 'So have ours. Sheep always are, by now, or hadn't you noticed?'

'Frankly, no. But you must see that these sheep are infinitely superior to any others – fairy-tale sheep. Any minute now neat-handed Phyllis will appear in quilted skirt with panniers and one of those straw hats with a ribbon, and Strephon in powdered hair and silk breeches, playing something Arcadian on a flute.'

'I can't wait to see Little Bo-Peep. But my darling, apart from sheep—'

Rodney pulled her down to a rustic bench and began to kiss her. She extricated herself reluctantly. 'Never mind sheep. I know you'd like to stay here all day, just doing nothing – except this sort of thing, of course – but we have a mission, a quest.'

'Have we? I thought we'd found what we were looking for.'

'A clock, darling, a clock. Remember?'

'Oh yes. I truly had forgotten. Is it so urgent?'

'Not if you want me to be arrested for aiding and

abetting a felony and receiving stolen goods. You could come and see me and we could talk through the wire with a wardress present, but somehow it wouldn't be quite the same. We're going to Honeyford House today, and early, before it gets too hot and sticky. If the clock's there then we've nothing to worry about, we can relax and enjoy ourselves.'

'How I hope it is.' Rodney looked wistful. 'Can we make this our HQ? I'd hate to move on.'

'I've asked Mrs Wilford already, and she said yes, practically with tears in her eyes. I could see her looking for confetti in my hair. She's probably given someone else the push to accommodate us. Now: Honeyford's on this side of Stratford, so what we do is make for Chipping Campden and get on to the A46 and cut across by back roads. At least they're back roads on the map. By now they've probably built a motorway.'

But nothing had changed. When they reached Chipping Campden at its southern end Doran slowed down to crawling pace. The long street lay before them, perfection in stone built over many centuries: little houses, grand houses, the seventeenth century calmly neighbouring the fifteenth, sixteenth and nineteenth, gables, oriels and door-canopies all harmonious. At the lovely Market Hall, four-square on its stone legs in mid-street, Doran parked.

'I don't care if it makes us a bit late. We're going to walk and look at the church and the ruins of Sir Baptist Hicks' house that Rupert's men burnt down to save it from Cromwell's lot. All that's left are the heavenly pavilions, or gazebos, or whatever, with little turrets, and next to them are Hicks's Almshouses that it would be a treat to die in, preferably live in. Come on.'

Rodney had started his clerical life in a Midland parish, but far over to the east, beyond Northampton. He had taken his dead wife to Stratford, but not through the Vale of Evesham. As they explored what he decided must be the most beautiful town in England he was silent from happiness, while Doran chattered for the same reason.

A bow-fronted shop window full of antique books made him lag behind her.

'I can't pass old book shops. You go on if you like.'

'I will! – I don't feel like frowsting this morning. I'll slip into the Grevel Arms and order some coffee, shall I?'

When Rodney joined her at the table overlooking the green he was carrying a parcel of books. 'They weren't dear, and I had to buy something today, just to show for it. And look, I found this.'

The booklet was almost fifty years old and tattered; it had been published before the war. But its yellowed pages had been preserved by a hard cover. Its title was *A Guide to Honeyford House, Warwickshire.* Doran almost snatched it.

'Darling, you're not only clever, you're inspired, brilliant. However did you come to notice this?'

'I've got a very good optician,' Rodney said modestly. 'Is it any use?'

She was turning the pages with the carefulness of one who handles old books like saints' relics. 'I'll say it is. There's a history, description, an inventory of contents – what about that? And photographs, look.'

He had hardly time to examine the sepia illustrations before she had taken the book and was running her finger down the pages of the inventory. She raised a triumphant face. 'It's here! There's even a picture. The description's not as detailed as it would be nowadays but it obviously refers to the same clock. If we drink this quickly we can be there well before lunchtime.'

A medieval bridge across the Avon, deep buttressed, doubtless to the gratification of foot travellers anxious not to get mown down by the farm-waggons which must once have taken up most of the bridge's width, brought them into Honeyford. Doran paused by the bridge-foot to allow a motor-coach to pass her. Impassive faces, presumably German, stared out of its windows. Doran watched it with disgust as it lumbered across the bridge, miraculously without demolishing the stones brushed by its bulging sides.

'Coaches! I only hope the monster's not going to the house.'

It was not, being bound for the church and the pub next door where a notice said Coaches Welcome. Doran followed a long narrow lane which brought them to high stone walls with an iron gate between them, falling off its hinges. A half-defaced board was almost illegible. Doran got out to read it.

'Honeyford House. This must be a side entrance. It also says *"Horses, Please Close the Gate".*'

'I'm sure the horses are always meticulous about closing it,' Rodney said.

But there were no horses to be seen in the shaggy field that may once have been a lawn. Beyond it was the house, Queen Anne to judge by its imposing front, much older by what could be seen of the rest of it, through overgrown trees.

'Oh!' exclaimed Doran. 'Where have the gardens gone?'

A balustraded terrace surrounded the house front. The steps leading up to it sprouted with weeds, and of the two eagle figures which had surmounted the newel posts only the lower halves survived, battered. What had been flower beds were wild tangles of shrubs and plants long since gone to seed, with here and there a malformed rose looking out of them. What might have been a small ornamental lake was choked with bulrushes, and an ornamental Gothic style conservatory was a skeleton, its coloured panes smashed.

'They weren't like this when we – when I was here last. Neglected, but not a wilderness. There was a gardener working, and the roses were just coming out.' She kicked aside a broken roof-tile which had fallen on to the path. 'If we walk round to the right we should come to the main entrance.'

'I'm afraid Time has got the garden, and the house too. Houses and gardens do die, without loving care,' said Rodney. 'This one looks as if it were coming to dust pretty rapidly.' They were at the portico, a crumbling structure obviously tacked on at some time to the original. A wire bell-pull hung beside the door, but when jerked produced no clangour. A handsome if rusted knocker failed to raise anyone. Rodney put his hand on the doorknob which turned.

'There's careless of somebody,' he said. 'We'd better go in and tell them – anybody could walk in.'

The large hall was darkly panelled, lit only by a window half-way up a fine staircase. High above them on the walls were hung broadswords, spears, helmets and a gloomy array of stags' skulls. There was a strong smell of what might have been dry rot or damp rot, or both, combined with the fustiness of a house seldom cleaned. Doran began to wish they had stayed outside; the whole enterprise suddenly seemed unlucky, the wrong errand to have undertaken on their happy day.

Out of the shadows by the staircase came a voice.

'Do you wish to see the house?'

As their eyes grew accustomed to the dimness they found themselves looking at a strange figure: a tiny woman, bent almost double, leaning on a cane, looking up at them under her eyelids in a way that chilled Rodney's blood. He remembered, uncomfortably, a moment in a ghost story when somebody comes upon a secret press that holds what seems at first to be a large mummified monkey, but wears the rags of a satin gown, and has strands of powdered hair clinging to its skull. The face of the old woman in the shadows had the appearance of having been crushed in a fist, like paper, so grotesquely crumpled it was.

Doran said, 'Lady Timberlake?'

'Do you wish to see the house?'

Doran raised her voice, going nearer. 'Lady Timberlake, you won't remember me, but I came here some years ago, and you kindly showed me round. I wonder if we might have a look round now?'

Whether the old creature heard her or not, a finger beckoned them into a room with the same look and smell of neglect. The walls were covered with pictures.

Lady Timberlake seemed to brighten and become less eldritch. 'So glad you could come,' said the tinny little voice. 'First you will want to see my greatest treasures, my dear husband's paintings. Here,' she gestured with her stick, 'is an early example, *The Regent's Canal in Winter*. Next, *Park Crescent, 1929*. Notice the use of cobalt.' In a slow shuffling progress she led them from one canvas to another, pointing and commenting.

'This is going to take all day,' Rodney whispered.

'It had better not,' Doran whispered back, pretending to pause at *Fitzroy Square, Morning*. 'They're all fakes. Utter daubs. The canvases aren't even stretched properly.'

'What are we going to do?'

'Leave it to me.' She raised her voice. 'Lady Timberlake, your husband's pictures are simply lovely. But I'm afraid we haven't very much time today – can we come back and look at them again? What we'd really like to see now are some of the treasures of the house. You had some charming small antique objects, I remember.'

Lady Timberlake shuffled closer to them. It became obvious that she personally contributed to the general miasma, which the heat of noon brought out overpoweringly. Rodney began to feel slightly sick and faint. As a priest he was used to unpleasant interior atmospheres, but something in this one was almost too much for him.

The old lady peered short-sightedly up at Doran. 'You – really – have not – the time. Pity, pity. Masterpieces, you know.'

'The other rooms,' Doran prompted, and led the way to a door she remembered. It took them into another unlit corridor where more stags' skulls stared down with dark eyeless sockets. From this they moved into a long, low-ceilinged room with an elaborate carved fireplace and some good furniture ranged round the walls. The pictures of the family who had originally owned the house were few and old, in heavy gilt frames. Lady Timberlake began to expound. 'This is the second baronet, 1625 to 1672. His wife, Lady Agatha. Sir Peregrine, imprisoned for allegiance to the King . . .'

Doran hissed at Rodney, 'Talk to her – keep her occupied, ask questions. I'm going to look for myself.' She darted off to a large glass-fronted cabinet in which porcelain figures and groups were displayed: too few exhibits, too many empty places where exhibits had stood. She remembered Meissen and early Derby, and some rare saltglaze. There were none now, only a few examples of Rockingham and a badly cracked piece of Bow. On the centre table – Italian mosaic, now with a nasty break in one corner – had stood a large, important pot-pourri bowl, *famille rose*. It was still there. So was a lovely marble figure of a goddess, under life-size, slightly mutilated but almost certainly Roman. But all the jewellery had vanished.

She examined the miniatures that bordered the fireplace. All early nineteenth-century or Victorian: where had the older ones gone, the Englehearts, the Cosways, an exquisite Carolean court lady by or after Samuel Cooper? The mantelpiece bore two Victorian lustres with many pieces missing, and a large clock of the same period.

Doran slipped into the next room, unnoticed. Lady Timberlake was now clinging confidently to Rodney's arm. In this room was part of a set of Chinese Chippendale chairs, a handsome George I bureau – and another Jacobean carved mantel. Looking over its contents, a pair of candlesticks, two poorish Minton vases, a couple of family photographs in silver frames, she knew with certainty that this was where the Edward East clock had stood. A glance at the old catalogue confirmed that it had been in this, the dining room.

She rejoined the others. Rodney was asking, 'And what happened to Sir Charles after the monarchy changed?' Doran interrupted,

'Lady Timberlake, I wonder if you've noticed that a very nice clock you used to have in the dining room has gone – a brass alarm, seventeenth-century? Perhaps you've moved it somewhere else.'

The crumpled face twitched, the hooded eyes blinked.

'Eh? No. I have no brass clocks.'

'But you used to have one. Look, in an old booklet about the house.'

For a long moment the old lady peered at the illustration, then muttered, 'Yes, yes, I recall that. Now where is it . . . ?'

'And,' Doran pressed on gently, 'several other things are not where they were when I was here last. Some good miniatures, quite a few pieces of porcelain, quite a bit of jewellery. One can see quite clearly where they've been. But perhaps you *have* moved them, or sold them.'

The old woman's mood had changed. The tiny body trembled all over and the stick was repeatedly banged on the floor. Rodney made appeasing noises, but the grey head was shaking furiously.

'I would not part with them. I would never sell them. *You*'ve taken them – you and him!' The stick pointed in accusation.

'Truly we haven't, Lady Timberlake. You must have had a lot of other people through the house—'

'All your accomplices! I see it all now, you're a gang of thieves, come to rob an old woman. You never even paid me to come in – fifty pence, fifty pence each, and you never gave me a penny. Help, help, police!' She began running about the room like a demented hen. Rodney and Doran looked desperately at each other.

'Let's go,' he said. 'I'm afraid she's mad.'

'We can't. This is serious. She really has been robbed. I think *we* ought to call the police, don't you?'

'And give our real names and identities, or false ones?' Rodney asked grimly.

'Oh. I hadn't thought of that – where's she gone?'

Lady Timberlake had vanished from the room. Far away they heard her shrieking 'Police, police!' Chasing her, they lost themselves in a warren of rooms and passages, until at last they found themselves in the kitchen quarters. The old woman was standing on tiptoe to reach a wall telephone, shouting into it.

'Yes, Lady Timberlake. Send your men at once. I've been robbed! I might be murdered before your men get here. Quick, hurry!'

Doran took Rodney's hand and led him into the cavernous, gloomy kitchen. She sat down at the filthy table, drawing him down beside her. 'Just keep quiet and still, and she'll calm down when she sees we're not trying to murder her to get away. Don't worry about the police. I'll give them my credentials and say you're just a friend. Leave it to me.'

Rodney kissed her hand. 'You're wonderful, and I love you very much indeed. And I wish we'd never come here.'

CHAPTER FOUR

*I could not see my table-spoons – I look'd, but could
   not see
The little fiddle-pattern'd ones I use when I'm at tea*

The police, when they arrived, proved anything but
formidable. A stout youngish sergeant, Thornboro,
who could have been a bit-part actor, and his constable, Partlett, black-avised enough to have been a
member of the Mafia, seemed not over-excited by the
prospect of an arrest. The two accused persons were
invited to step down to the station for a chat, but
neither felt seriously menaced.

   They had arranged in swift private conference what
to say. Doran frankly gave her name, address, and
professional details, and the telephone numbers of her
bank manager, Ernest Tilman, and a very prestigious
gallery owner in Jermyn Street. Mr Barham was just, er, a
friend. Her soft tone and the warm glance she stole at
him convinced Sergeant Thornboro that their connection was purely romantic. She had removed the wedding
ring. Without make-up, glowing with heat and the
morning's sunshine, Doran looked about eighteen, while
Rodney, in jeans and a Marks and Spencer sports shirt,
might have been any youngish man out with his girlfriend. He blessed the heavy horn-rims which lent an
owlish, learned air such as trendier spectacles would not
have bestowed, besides, he thought, giving him an
endearing resemblance to Harold Lloyd.

'I'd heard about Honeyford House,' Doran confided to the sergeant over thick cups of station tea. 'I visited it once or twice with school parties – I lived in Oxford. And a few years ago, when I was at university, I remember thinking there were some marvellous things in the house. And now, today – I saw that a lot had obviously gone. Lady Timberlake *may* have sold them, of course.'

'Not she. All she sold were pictures her husband did.'

'You know, then – about the fakes?'

'We do, miss. It's an open secret round here. She got rid of the lot about six years ago when she had a good offer, and paid some pavement artist to make rough copies of them, so that she'd have something of Sir Gerald about the house. She was very fond of her husband, was Lady T., in spite of the way he let her down.'

'He ran off with a model, didn't he?' asked Doran innocently.

'That's right. Not long after he'd been knighted for painting a lot of what you might call civic pictures, lord mayors and Whitehall people. I don't remember it myself, of course, but people said the old King, that was King George V, was very put out about it, and said the bug . . . – the gentleman ought to have handed his knighthood back. Specially as it wasn't the first model Sir Gerald had, er, played around with.'

'Really. No wonder Lady Timberlake is rather strange in her manner.'

'Strange, miss? She's barmy, potty, right round the twist. Everybody knows her. Ought to be taken into care, some say, but she does no harm except to herself, and there's no action we can take about the house, seeing as it's in private hands.'

'Can't you make her see that she mustn't leave the front door open? Anybody could walk in. We did.'

'We've tried, don't think we haven't. I took it to the

top, myself, and they sent a WPC up from Cheltenham to make her see reason. But you might as well talk to the moon, and now you say there's a lot of her things vanished. Speaking of which, miss, if you could give me a list . . . ?'

Doran was thankful for the old catalogue, which saved her from appearing to have too much fore-knowledge. Remarking that she now knew what should have been in the house, and was not, she ticked off various items on the inventory, carefully drawing no special attention to the clock. She was startled to see how much had gone, and of what high quality. The person or persons who had removed the articles had known what they were doing.

Thornboro thanked her profusely. 'And don't you worry, Miss Fairweather, there won't be any repercussions. It's quite clear to me that you had nothing to do with the matter, except to bring it to our attention. We did phone your two friends, by the way, and they both said to give you their best regards.'

'Kind of them. If you could be so obliging as to drive us back to the house now, I'll pick up my car. There's just one thing worrying me – that Lady Timberlake will still be there, in quite some danger. Isn't there anything to be done? I'll talk to her myself, if you like.'

The susceptible sergeant reflected that she was not only very pretty, in an unusual, delicate sort of way, reminding him of a young dancer he had fallen for once when the ballet came to Stratford, but that she had a beautiful nature. He hoped that the serious-looking Mr Barham would take care of her and not play her false, with the awful example of Gerald Timberlake before his eyes.

'Don't you trouble about that for a minute, miss. We've got the phone number of a niece of hers, that told us she'd come over any time if the old lady seemed to need her. I'll give her a call now, while the constable's taking you back.'

They parted on almost affectionate terms. 'If that was life at the nick,' Rodney said when they were alone again, 'I could get quite a taste for it.'

'So could I, except for the tea. And I am here to tell you that I am dreadfully, shockingly, savagely hungry. I could eat polythene and putty, mixed, and drink paint-stripper.'

'Then, my darling, we'll either drive to the nearest builder's merchants or to Stratford, where I know for a fact one can get a substantial meal at practically any hour of the day.'

Stratford supplied them with a meal that was certainly substantial – Doran had never expected to enjoy fried fish, chips, and peas followed by something described as Mistress Anne's Apple Pie and ice cream, eaten at three in the afternoon. They ate with almost silent concentration, then walked off the effects in Stratford's thronged streets.

'Pity about all this,' Rodney said. 'Those things like striped humbugs were once decent Georgian front-ages. But no, that wouldn't do for tourism.'

'There used to be proper shops, selling useful things. Now they sell everything no normal person could possibly want, from yards of tartan to plastic Beefeater dolls made in Taiwan.'

They passed the top of Henley Street and looked along it at the serried ranks of coaches. Rodney said, 'Let's not go and see the Birthplace, shall we? The Bard wouldn't know it, anyway. Since his time it's been a butcher's shop.'

'And a pub.'

'That's right, the Swan and Maidenhead. The Bard would have made something bawdy of it. Leda in Henley Street. No, I don't want to see the Birthplace, definitely. Keats wrote his name on the wall, and some foul vandal whitewashed it over, curse him.'

'If I might just lead back the conversation towards Shakespeare,' said Doran, 'I think we ought to talk

60

about the clock question, which is why we come to be here at all. I personally am tired of walking about in this sticky heat, and I suggest we take ourselves into New Place Gardens and sit on a seat in the shade.'

In that blessed retreat from the world they were lucky enough to find the little arbour among the flowers which is always cool, and for some reason not popular with tourists, unoccupied.

'About the Shakespeare connection with the clock,' Doran said. 'I did look it up at home, and there it was in the useful Honeyford catalogue. Pity I had to leave it with that nice copper, but I can remember. Elizabeth Hall, Shakespeare's granddaughter, married twice. She was Lady Barnard when she made her will in 1670, and left a fair bit of property and a lot of money for those times. One of the legacies was fifty pounds each to four daughters of her kinsman Thomas Hathaway – Joan, Elizabeth, Susanna and Rose. That's the name on the backplate of the clock. Rose Hathaway.'

'Rose. Charming name. The Bard mentions roses more than a hundred times – did you know? – even names over eight varieties.'

'Does he, indeed?' Doran patted his knee. 'Well, that's all the will says, except that Joan was married and the others weren't. Rose could have been a special favourite, and been given this very handsome modern clock. Perhaps all the sisters got presents.'

'Does it make the clock more valuable – Rose's name?'

'Alas no, not without a provenance, saying where it's been and in whose hands. A provenance is what the Trade calls any document authenticating the object, giving dates and signatures and things, a sort of birth certificate. After all, anyone could get an engraver to put a famous name on something. It's called sclentering.'

'I should have thought Shakespeare would be a bit more of a seller than Hathaway. Why not sclenter him?'

'My sweet innocent, it's been done, rather often. But

his dates don't fit with the clock. Anyway, there were hundreds of Shakespeares all over Warwickshire. Probably old Lady T. could have supplied a provenance, but she's too far over the hill now. Leaving aside the clock – it looks to me as though we've got a major steal on our hands. Did you notice all those items I ticked off for the police?'

'There seemed to be a lot.'

'There were, and worth thousands and tens of thousands, added up. All valuable, some immensely valuable, all rare, all small and portable. The big, awkward things I remembered were still there.' Doran gazed out across immaculate flower beds, kaleidoscopes of blooms planted with mathematical precision. 'I wonder whether one person lifted them, or whether Honeyford House turned into a free-for-all.'

'From what I've heard of your unscrupulous trade, my love, I should have thought there'd have been frantic in-fighting if more than one thief had been concerned.'

'There would – blood all over the parquet. No, my guess is that one or two people did the stealing – probably two, first one, then the other. They could even have used a child – children are fashionable in shoplifting circles, I hear.'

'Do you think these were just any old robbers, as it were Burglar Bill or Sam the Swagman?' asked Rodney.

'Quite definitely not. They couldn't have shifted stuff like that, or had the knowledge to pick it out in the first place.'

'So it could have been . . . someone like Howell?'

Doran shook her head vehemently. 'Impossible. I had some nasty doubts, but Howell would never have had the sheer brass nerve to move all that. The clock he might have pinched, because he's mad on them, but not the rest. Besides, that thieving's been done over a period of time, and he's never been away that long.' She jumped to her feet. 'I feel twitchy – let's stroll.'

They walked slowly along the paths, pausing at the Shakespeare statue. 'They couldn't think where else to put it, so they shoved it against a hedge, in a corner,' Rodney said. 'Typical Stratford, in a way.'

Their arms were linked in spite of the late afternoon heat and stickiness. A sensation of faint melancholy had come over Rodney, and something like apprehension. There was going to be an investigation, perhaps a chase, which might well lead to disclosures and trouble. At Honeyford he had got away lightly by saying little and looking anonymous, but if the waters got deeper he might have to admit his identity.

He was not quite sure what he had hoped for: perhaps that Doran would find the clock in its proper place. There would have been no mystery, and they could have embarked on a carefree unofficial honeymoon. That was impossible now. A sense of guilt nagged him, though he thought he had sensibly talked himself out of it. Whatever God might have decided to do about his conscience, it was still there, an invisible dog collar tightening about his neck.

There was another worry. 'You won't,' he said, 'do anything rash, will you, like barging into the dens of sinister Orientals, or taking on seven-foot bruisers single-handed? You did get knocked about rather nastily last year, investigating things.'

'Me? Why should I do anything rash? I'm simply going to ask questions. I thought we'd drive back to Honeyford and sample any likely pubs. Somebody's bound to know about local dealers; they're great ones for pub-haunting, especially when there's an auction.'

The car was in a particularly unattractive public park, jammed among hundreds of others and the ubiquitous coaches. Doran opened the doors to let out the heat, and stood looking towards the theatre. On its red roof the yellow flag hung slack, the falcon rested from shaking its spear. Behind, round the river's curve, the spire of Holy Trinity rose against a clear blue sky. 'This place is magic,' she said. 'Pity about all the vulgarity, fish and chips and pizza parlours and demolition and frightful souvenirs and, I gather, productions with no scenery and characters in boiler suits. But it's still magic. I wonder why?'

'The Bard, I suppose. He was magic. Some people are – you are.'

'Flatterer.'

'But others are decidedly not. For instance . . .'

On a roundabout route to Honeyford, to ensure that the pubs would be open when they got there, Rodney discoursed on the magic and non-magic qualities of their acquaintances and various persons of history, drawing various odd conclusions, such as that Hitler was magic but the wrong sort, and that only three of the Stuarts were magic in spite of family reputation.

They arrived at the nearest inn to Honeyford at five minutes after opening time, six o'clock, and confidently entered it. Its small bar parlour was crowded to the doors. All the punk youth of the Warwickshire borders seemed to have dropped in and been immediately served. A shifting tapestry of pink, green, blue and orange spiked heads emitted a roar of chatter, from which the two newcomers could deduce a vocabulary restricted but forceful.

'Anglo-Saxon attitudes, Anglo-Saxon dialogue,' Rodney shouted above the din. 'Come on, it's impossible in here.'

'How did they get there, in the time?' Doran asked outside. 'They must have been leaning up against the door and stormed the place.'

'Like the Bastille. Did you know that when the Revolutionary troops stormed the Bastille they only found seven old men inside, two of them Irish? They were most annoyed at being disturbed.'

'Disappointing for all concerned. Let's try the next pub.'

The George, on the river, was also full, but of tourists

who had arrived in a private coach and twenty-three cars. One harassed barmaid was attempting to serve a party of white-haired ladies from Leeds and a number of baffled Americans. All hope of an enlightening chat about the local dealers was fading from Doran's mind when a progress through the Red Lion, Three Jackdaws, and Angel and Crown brought them to the Queen's Head. There, beneath a grim-faced effigy of the first Elizabeth, they found a bar empty but for a couple playing darts and a man reading the evening paper with his beer.

'I think we've struck oil,' Doran said quietly. 'Look what's behind the bar.'

A woman in her early thirties was languidly polishing glasses. Her expensively cut and high-lighted hair, rinsed copper-gold, and a silk shirt which might as well have worn its designer label on the outside, proclaimed her no mere barmaid. Her manicured hands sparkled with rings: Doran, reminded, put back her own status ring on to her finger, with difficulty. The ring was a size too small.

Rodney whispered, ' "Is not mine hostess of the tavern a most sweet wench?" '

'Sweet, perhaps, bored, certainly.' Doran approached the bar. 'Good evening.'

The vision looked up. 'Good evening.' Her voice was pure Sloane. Rodney ordered two spritzers and embarked on a routine of chat about the heat, the roads and the visitors. The languid lady warmed, accepted a spritzer herself, and volunteered the information that she found Warwickshire pub life a total drag. 'We came here from Fulham. Something gave us the idea that it would be gorgeous to run a sweet pub in the country. My God! Little did we think.'

'Sydney Smith,' Rodney mused, 'described the country as a kind of healthy grave.'

'I do see what he meant, whoever he may be. No one to talk to, nothing to do, except hand out drinks in this bloody bar – and they all drink the bloody same, anyway. I rather fancied myself at mixing cocktails, but what a hope.'

Doran sympathized, and led the conversation round to visitors from London, while unobtrusively studying a picture on the wall near the bar. It was a composition of needlework and paint, showing an exotic bird with pale feathers and ruby eyes in a landscape of once-brilliant flowers and trees.

'That's nice,' she said. 'I expect you get a lot of people admiring it?'

'Not really, rather dull for their taste. Just something we brought with us - my mama had a set of them but they got split up, you know how it is.'

'Too well. I hope you take care of it, because it's eighteenth-century French and beautifully done. I expect you know it's got a bit of moth.'

'No! Where?' Their hostess came round the bar and examined the picture. 'Oh dear. Now you mention it, we did have someone wanting to buy it, not too long ago. I said no, of course, its part of our own décor, as distinct from the awful brewer's ads we have to display. Yes, he was quite pressing, and he liked those horse-brasses, too.'

Doran touched the dark leather, lifted one of the brasses, weighing it in her hand. 'I should think he would. It's an unusually nice martingale, and the castings are early Victorian. They have a completely different feel from the copies, and the backs give the whole thing away. That's a Midland Railway commemorative, the little engine – 1844.'

'Aren't you clever! Can you tell me about our other brasses?'

'Yes, they're rubbish, you can buy them from iron-mongers.'

'Actually we did. You *are* clever. Are you in the business?'

'I dabble,' Doran said modestly. 'I suppose you have a lot of dealers round here?'

'I never really noticed. There are some empty shops. Oh, and there's Taddeus. Tony Taddeus, know him?'

'The name rings a bell. What's he like?'

'Oh, I dunno, hard to describe, except not my type. Sort of fortyish, dark, going thin on top, could have been Greek to start with. We don't see a lot of him because he isn't what you might call pubbable. He did come in last week, now I think of it, with some pal or other – that's right, he was the one who asked about the picture – and they had some of our hot food.' She indicated a blackboard showing Dishes of the Day.

'Do you happen to remember what the friend was like?' Doran asked. Rodney knew that she was expecting, fearing, the description of a short dark man with a strong Welsh accent. But the landlady shook her head. 'Sorry. It was a busy day. My husband might remember.' She shouted into the other bar. 'Jeremy!' A companion piece to herself appeared: he might have been an older relative of our Royal Princes. Yes, he said he had noticed Tony Taddeus with someone. He seemed to recall a grey-haired man, tall and thin, who had been talking a lot until he, Jeremy, approached the table with their meal, on which he had shut up like a clam, not even said thank you. 'One remembers that kind of thing,' Jeremy said. 'Customers don't have to be fulsome, just civil – we don't ask a lot, do we, Sue?'

'No indeed, darling. These lovely people have been so nice to me. I could kiss them. At any rate, you,' she directed at Rodney, who smiled but backed imperceptibly.

Doran said, 'Sorry to grill you, but I think this man must have been a friend of mine. Do you happen to remember if there was anything about his mouth that struck you at all?'

'Well, now you mention it, yes. It turned right down

at the corners – like this.' He went to the menu blackboard and with chalk drew a caricature sketch of a face in which the mouth-line was an inverted half-moon.

'That's him,' Doran said. 'How very interesting. I must tell him all about coming here when I see him next. Oh, and he has a rather off-putting manner, but it's just shyness. Thank you so much for being helpful. We've so much enjoyed dropping in.'

With cordial farewells they left Sue and Jeremy. The dart players had begun another game, and the man with the newspaper had reached the sporting pages.

'What on earth . . . ?' Rodney began as they walked back to the car.

'Vic Maidment. Remember? A friend of Howell's and an utter – let's call it swine. I know stronger and more suitable terms, but why should I sully my lips with them? Equally, of course, why should I slander pigs? He *has* an off-putting manner but it isn't shyness, it's sheer bloodymindedness. I've met some nasty dealers but he's the bottom of the pack. Well, almost. And we know he was cut in on the clock deal, don't we.'

'So what do we do – go back to Eastgate and cross-question him?'

'We don't. He wasn't there on Sunday or Monday and I wouldn't know where to find him. No, we're not going back to Eastgate. I'm certain there's more to be unearthed round here.'

'Would you say Maidment was a dangerous man – violent?'

Doran, manoeuvring the car into the main road, considered.

'How can one tell? I've never seen him exhibit signs of violence at a sale, or in the Port Arms. He doesn't drink a lot, or if he does it's at home. I once beat him over a jug that was being sold as doubtful Worcester and turned out to be very good Liverpool, probably Seth Pennington, which I knew it was. He didn't turn and bite me, just ill-wished me as hard as he could. Probably went home and stuck pins into a wax effigy of me.'

'Doesn't sound anyone's favourite man. Look, don't you think all this has gone far enough? The police know about the thefts – why not leave it with them?'

'Because the clock comes into it, and if they follow that trail they'll probably arrive at Howell.'

'So? Can't he take the rap for his own misdeeds? You could make it clear that you had nothing to do with it, personally.'

'I don't think he could take the rap. If he got found out in anything as big as this he might very well disintegrate. Darling, I've never said a lot to you about Howell, but he's a pathetic creature apart from his business acumen and a lot of flair for his own sort of stuff. He drinks, and he's on drugs, though how much I don't know, or what kind – only that he smokes joints, and sometimes he's very strange in the mornings. He's got a dodgy background: his father was a miner who went savage when the pit closed and he was out of work, which seemed to be for years on end. Howell and his mother both got beaten up regularly. So you see, there's a lot of allowance to be made.'

'You're taking a thoroughly Christian attitude to your chum,' said Rodney, 'and I should stand duly reproved and shut up about it. But if I had a pound for every parishioner and non-parishioner I've come across who'd had a dodgy, even hellish, background, I should be rolling in riches by now – and most of them have turned out very well.'

'Here endeth the First Lesson.'

'Sorry. I know I'm on holiday and I shouldn't. But it makes me mad, you running yourself into danger because of Howell Evans.'

Doran said nothing. A few minutes later she exclaimed with annoyance, 'Damn, I've taken the wrong turning and we're heading for Evesham. I'll go back when we come to a side road.'

'Don't bother.' He was consulting the map. 'There's a right turn out of Evesham that'll take us back towards Chipping. Look at that lovely house.'

'I can't, I'm watching the road.'

'Then stop – it's worth it.' Doran obeyed.

'Dilapidated, but what a wonderful hotch-potch of the centuries,' Rodney said. 'A lot of Elizabethan, some Jacobean, and what looks like a little farmhouse, and a bit of a moat. Mariana's house, the Moated Grange. Perhaps the Bard was thinking of it when he wrote *Measure for Measure*. It's so near Stratford.'

'I'd like to have the furnishings of it,' Doran mused. 'I could go mad with triple folky (that's country furniture and particularly old oak to you, love) for the Tudor bits, and the Jacobean. I adore it, but I haven't much room for it at Bell. Instead of selling desirables I could bring them up here: court cupboards and joint stools and turner-made chairs and shepherds' chairs and *deuddarns,* proper ones from Wales, and those androgynes they used to have on four-posters and carved chimney pieces . . . '

'Who'd live in the house, with all this triple folky? You?'

'No, us. Us, please.' They both thought of themselves in the romantic house, idyllically alone. Only they wouldn't be alone. There would still be Helena.

Doran sighed and changed the subject. 'Well, if it *was* Mariana's house she ought to have kept busy polishing and worm-hunting, instead of mooning after that berk Angelo. Lots of wives are deserted – and he didn't take the house. I've never believed in the ending of *Measure*, you know.'

'Nor have I. At least, I'm not sure. It's a deeply Christian play. Perhaps Mariana truly forgave him, even though he'd abandoned her.'

'Or perhaps she just fancied him, berk or not.

70

Anyway, she was a rotten housewife – creaking hinges and flies singing on the window-panes, indeed. Well, never mind – if I had that particular moated grange I'd furnish it just to amuse myself – us. And the ghosts.'

Rodney was turning the pages of an old guidebook. 'Yes, it's mentioned here. The book says, "It has a strange mysterious charm, perhaps that of old loyalties or old plottings . . . " ' He shut the book and gazed at the house.

Doran said gently, 'You're getting melancholy. Cheer up. There's nothing to worry about.'

'No, of course not. Except that I must find a telephone box before it gets much later. Not that Arline's likely to be tucked up yet.'

There was a box outside a post office a mile or two on. Doran watched him at the telephone with a feeling of unrest, almost anger. The memory of their idyll of the night before had been bruised a little by the encounter with the police and the risk of Rodney's identity being brought into the open. Now it was being broken into by his renewing contact with Helena. Of course he must make sure that she had settled down, was not ill or giving trouble. Of course he must send her a message of love and reassurance. It would be inhuman to expect him to do anything else. For he did love his unhappy daughter, with a love that was quite different from the love he shared with Doran, and very strong. Strong enough to keep him from marrying.

He rejoined her. 'All right?' she asked.

'Fine. Helena's been in bed all day, resting after the long drive. The people there seem perfectly capable of looking after her. Or so I infer, since Arline's been swimming, playing squash, and walking round the bay on the cliffs.'

'Oh. Good.'

The evening was closing in on them, stars coming out in a darkening sky, the stones of Evesham under

71

their wheels and its two church towers ahead. Suddenly Doran exclaimed, 'Would you believe? I'm on the wrong road again – we're heading for Tewkesbury.'

'Then let's go to Tewkesbury. We could see the bones of false, fleeting, perjur'd Clarence and Warwick's fair daughter Isobel.'

'Not at this time of night, surely. Anyway, they're not on view, are they?'

'They are, if you ask someone, in a glass case in the vaults, because the river rose and the tombs were getting swamped. I saw them once when I was cathedraling. They're all mingled together, his and hers, one in death as in life, little delicate Plantagenet bones.'

Doran shivered. 'What's the Chipping road number? There's a torch in the glove compartment.'

Rodney searched, and scanned the map. 'B4035, it looks like.'

About to turn the car at an entrance drive, she said, 'Look over there, to the west, on the skyline. That's Bredon Hill.'

'Bredon. Summertime on – ?'

'The same.'

As they looked towards the dark outline the same tune went through their minds, the tune of the sad English song. Doran said, 'I'm cold. Let's go home.'

Rodney did not ask whether she meant Abbotsbourne. Their only home, in their brief time together, was the Leaping Trout Inn. This bed thy centre is, these walls thy sphere.

CHAPTER FIVE

. . . as dead as any nail that is in any door

'That's Dover's Hill over there.' Rodney pointed, from the grassy eminence on which they were standing, high above the Trout's chimneys. 'It's where the three counties meet – Warwickshire, Worcestershire, and Gloucestershire.'

'Hence the name Dover, I presume.'

'Not at all. Mr Dover was a lawyer and a bit of a health nut, not to mention a Puritan reactionary. In the 1630s he decided to attract people away from the pubs by putting on outdoor games, sort of Cotswold Olympics'.

'On that hill?'

'That, and thereabouts. There's mention of a plain, and swains with belts and silk handkerchiefs, and nymphs in straw hats and tawdry ribands. Ben Johnson was there, and a tremendous Royalist called Endymion Porter, who came from Aston Subedge and dressed with Spanish elegance. The Games went on until the middle of last century, when they were stopped because of murder, disorder and raping.'

'Rodney, I know you're extremely erudite,' said Doran, 'but you're simply showing off. Don't tell me you knew all this before we came here, because I shan't believe you.'

'Well, no. There are some very perusable books in the residents' parlour, and I had a good read while you were in the kitchen rabbiting on with Mrs Wilford and that nice Betty.'

'I was only asking her about recipes. She's got some interesting local ones.' Doran kept to herself her hope that she might learn to cook, for what cookery she was capable of at present would not be good enough for Rodney. They were at the top of the hill now, looking down on coloured counties stretching as far as the eye could see: golden fields waiting for harvesting, green fields pallid with summer heat, starred with languid sheep, ribbons of ancient hedgerow and knots of trees. In two hundred, perhaps three hundred years the landscape had not changed greatly. Doran sighed with the peace of it, and kicked off her shoes to feel the short warm prickly grass under her feet. Compelled by a contrary impulse, she glanced at her watch. It was ten o'clock. She sighed again, this time with regret.

'We ought to be setting off, I suppose.'

Rodney did not ask 'Where?' knowing very well. Instead he said: 'I had a dream last night, that I was clutching you very tightly, in a sort of stranglehold.'

'How delightful. But I don't think you can have been, because it would have wakened me – not that I should have minded.'

'Well, I knew the reason for it, as one sometimes does in dreams. It wasn't just the obvious reason – it was to keep you safe, to stop you going away from me. I'll do it again, now.' He pulled her close, and they stood embraced. He tilted up her face to kiss her, and saw from her smiling eyes that she was not getting any message from his words. 'I'm not going away from you,' she said. 'Just try to get rid of me.'

Having failed with Plan One, Rodney switched to Plan Two.

'I imagine you want to go back to Honeyford this morning. Right. I was looking at the map after breakfast, and I thought we'd go a different route and take in Broadway, before quite all the ten thousand coaches

74

have arrived. I've never been there, if you can believe that, so you can see all my local lore is purely theoretical. And you could look at the antique shops – the guide says the place is stiff with them.'

Doran snorted. 'You're jesting, of course. Top class, top prices, dealers who know it all and wouldn't be interested in my pathetic chequebook. Still, we could just *look,* I suppose . . . '

They looked in every antique-shop window of the lush picture-postcard village, Doran lingering wistfully over costly bric-a-brac and fine furniture. In one dark interior she spotted an object which drew her into the shop. It was the figure, painted on board and rather less than life-size, of a little girl in the costume of Queen Anne's day, a lace fontange like a cockerel's comb crowning the rosy demure face. 'I must have it,' Doran said, vanishing purposefully.

She came out shaking her head. 'Absolutely hopeless. The earth, and all the riches of Ind. Couldn't be done, and I feel bereaved.'

'What is it?'

'A dummy board, fireplace screen, end-of-seventeenth-century, meant to stand in front of the empty grate in summer. Mostly made by out-of-work sign painters. I wanted it for myself, not for stock. Can't you see it in Bell House?'

Rodney could, and wished he could have walked into the shop and bought it for his love. They had used up as much time as he had hoped in Broadway, but his plan of postponement was not yet perfected. A brisk petition for extra time (They must certainly be on his side) took the car down a lane slightly off their route, and past a cottage whose front wall had been turned into a shop window. Above it was painted *Antiques and Curios. Melody Lee.* Doran stopped the car and Rodney sketched a salute in the direction of heaven.

'Look,' she said, excited, 'a gorgeous mess of absolute

rubbish, but you never know. Just a quick root through, and then we press on.'

They were barely inside the shop before the presumed owner shot out from behind a bead curtain at the back. Her black hair hung long and uncombed over her shoulders, and her skin was of the colour and texture of tanned leather. Her scarlet lipstick had been lavishly applied, more or less matching the shapeless and heavily stained garment she wore, which stopped short to show old plaid carpet-slippers.

'You wanner look round?' she asked, and it would have seemed quite natural if she had added 'pretty lady and gentleman'. Her accent was unplaceable, veering towards Cockney. Doran politely agreed, adding that she was Trade, and flourishing her card. Melody Lee's nutlike face took on a curious expression which might have meant that she was interested, suspicious, disapproving, delighted, or all four. Not one given to childlike trust, Rodney thought as she settled down on a stool to watch them, fag in mouth.

Doran was not tempted by Melody Lee's collection of imitation Goss china, plaster objects in the rough likenesses of Marilyn Monroe and the late Sir Winston Churchill, miscellaneous small silver, wedding rings with who knew what sad history, and second-hand clothes giving off their peculiarly musty odour. A few nasty figurines on a shelf imitated Bow and Dresden porcelain; they were produced wholesale in Hong Kong, and were the sort of objects which went well in Doran's Eastgate shop during the tourist season, when she could bring herself to stock them.

Rodney, sorting through a tray, found a Victorian silver brooch bearing the name Helena. The pin was bent, but it could be straightened, and he thought it would please his child. Melody Lee's boot-button eyes were fixed on him, as he examined it, waiting for him to pocket it without paying. About to approach her, money in hand, he saw Doran freeze.

She was standing quite still, holding one of the figurines. It had not, even Rodney knew, been made in Hong Kong, from the glimpse he had of it before Doran put it down and stepped back to survey it.

On the back of a horse about twelve centimetres high, with a long curved neck like a snake's, sat two tiny people, a man in a cocked hat and tight-fitting jacket, authoritatively holding the reins, and his wife riding pillion, her waist impossibly slender and her full skirts spreading over the horse's rump. Doran asked, 'Do you know anything about this?'

Melody Lee's face became sphinxlike. 'Much as you do, I 'spect.'

'Well, can you remember where it came from?'

'I never remembers. Things just come.'

'What can you do me on it?'

A pause, then 'For'y pahnds.'

'A bit over the top for me, I'm afraid. Can't you do better than that? Its badly damaged, you know – one of the horse's ears is off, there's a crack in the off hind leg, and the girl's right arm's been clumsily repaired. It's not worth anything like that to me. I can't sell it as a perfect piece, and you know what repairs do to value.'

'You 'eard what I said, missis.'

Doran appeared to muse. 'I've seen something awfully like it before – I wonder where? Can you remember, darling?' She turned to Rodney, with a look full of meaning which he rightly interpreted. 'Don't, don't!' said his answering look. 'There's something wrong here – don't get mixed up in it.' But she shook her head slightly and turned back to the gipsy.

'Well, it's a lot of money for a wreck, but I like it. You'll take a cheque, I suppose?

'Nah. I been 'ad that way too often. I don't take no kites these days, missis.'

'I promise you it's not a bad cheque, Mrs Lee. I'll give you a number to ring, if you don't believe me – my bank manager.' A dirty, old-fashioned telephone handset was on a desk in the corner. Doran smiled inwardly to think how startled Ernest Tilman was going to be to get yet another call about her from the Cotswold outback – if the call was ever made, but somehow she doubted that it would be. Melody Lee was now openly on the defensive.

'You think I'm screwin' you up, that it? Well, I ain't, and you're not goin' to screw me up neither. I wants cash for that piece, or it don't go out of my shop, see. Dunno you from Adam, do I.'

'You've seen my trade card. Isn't that enough?'

The gipsy shrugged. 'I been cleaned out too often. Anyone can 'ave a card printed.'

'Do you really think, darling—' Rodney began, but Doran was snapping her bag firmly and hitching it back on her shoulder. 'All right, cash,' she said. 'I'll bring it round early tomorrow morning and you can have the piece wrapped up ready for me, OK?'

Melody Lee hesitated, then nodded. Raking Doran's face with her eyes, she muttered, 'You watch out for the red stones, my fine young *chai* with yer fake ring and yer fancy man.' Rodney put down the price of the brooch, took Doran's arm, and almost pulled her out of the shop.

'What on earth was all that about? There's something fishy about that piece, isn't there? Come on, what is it?'

'Fishy? It's not a wrong 'un, if you mean that. It's earthenware, slipware, very early Staffs., Astbury-Whieldon type, and there's something very, very like it in Brighton Museum.' She paused. 'And it was one of the items that had gone from Honeyford House.'

The sound of the Volvo was out of hearing down the lane. The little shop of Melody Lee was silent but for the mutter of her voice. Another voice said down the earpiece of the dusty telephone: 'You stupid bloody bitch.'

'You won't collect that thing in the morning, of course.'

Doran raised her eyebrows. 'But of course I shall. It's evidence, isn't it? I know what it is and where it came from, and I can prove it, with the catalogue the police have. It's stolen goods, and how it got into that woman's hands I don't know, but I'm going to trace it back to whoever stole it from Lady T.'

Rodney said tersely, 'There's a pub. You can park round the side. I'm not going to discuss this while you're driving, so don't argue. Left turn, and get in next to that Rover, where there's a bit of shade.'

Doran shot him a surprised glance. 'I hear and obey, O my lord and master. Do you know, I rather like being ordered about.'

They found places in the sun on the pub patio, to which Rodney brought two halves of cider and four sandwiches. 'Now,' he said, 'just what are you planning to do?'

'Find this man Taddeus and ask him what he knows about it.'

'You're quite sure he's the connection?'

'Well, not *sure* – but it seems so likely, with him having been seen about with Vic Maidment.'

'Couldn't Maidment simply have been on a whatsit, a buying trip?'

'He could, but it's a bit of a coincidence, and I tend not to believe in coincidence, do you?'

'Never mind my views on Fate. You don't even know that Maidment's criminally involved with the theft of the clock.'

Doran sighed patiently. 'I don't *know*, but I do know there was a theft, and Vic's got connections everywhere. Receivers, I mean, though nowadays they don't talk about fences and receivers – it's "dishonestly handling". And what about that landlord in the George,

79

drawing that sketch of Vic's face? I asked him about the mouth on an impulse, call it inspiration if you like, and you see I was right.'

'So what do you intend to do?'

'Go and see Taddeus, of course. But you know that.'

'Darling love, don't you think you read too much detective fiction?'

'Rubbish. I don't take it seriously. I just like novels that are about something, not people going on and on at each other about their awful sex lives. It's either that, or they're slowly dying of something disgusting, or else they're foreigners one can't quite believe in and doesn't care about anyway, or one's expected to plough through some interminable historical novel with people pointing out to each other details they wouldn't even have thought twice about, like, "By the Mass: Here cometh a wight clad in doublet and hose . . . " '

Rodney put his hand over hers. 'Doran. Don't waffle, and don't try to put me off. I'm not a bit keen on barging into this man's shop and bringing the conversation cunningly round to what he had to do with the Honeyford thefts. It could get us into bad trouble. I'm quite serious, you know. Telephone, if you must make contact with him.'

'And say what, pray?'

'Say you've heard of him through the Trade and you'd be interested to meet him – and take it from there.'

When Doran made her eyes glow the ring of brown in them shone like a tiny bronze chaplet, and the seagreen-blue of the irises seemed deep enough to drown a man. 'You're wonderful,' she said, 'as clever as you're attractive, seductive, gorgeous, in fact devastating. Why haven't I realized that before?'

'Perhaps,' Rodney replied seriously, 'because we've stopped play-acting with each other. Now, are you going to telephone Taddeus?'

'Yes. If you say so. Anyway, I believe you're right. I don't think I can finish this sandwich, it's plastic. Rodney . . . what did that woman, Melody Lee, mean by what she said as we were going out? I rather thought it implied that my wedding ring wasn't real and that you weren't my husband. Now how could she possibly have known that?'

' "Old Meg she was a gipsy." Not much doubt of that – "an old red blanket cloak she wore", precisely as Keats said. Gipsies do know things, even if a lot of it's fake. I'm inclined to believe this was genuine. She said something else, too – that you were to beware or watch out for red stones. Remember that, will you?'

'Yes. Though I can't think what it meant. Terracotta? Red sandstone? And I don't care for having magic, or the Sight, or whatever, used on me. Yuck. I suppose I ought to have crossed her palm with silver. Well, if I'm going to telephone I might as well do it now – twelve-fifteen, a fair enough before-lunch time, wouldn't you think?'

Rodney stood by listening to one side of the conversation, and holding ten-penny pieces to feed the pay phone. Doran hung up and turned to him, thoughtful-faced.

'Well, it doesn't sound particularly sinister. That was his wife – he's away till tomorrow. She says she's sure he'd like to meet me and suggested tomorrow evening, if he's back in time and free. I said all right. She's calling back at the Trout about six tomorrow. It's putting things off, but I can't do anything about it, can I? You were absolutely on the ball, making me telephone.'

'Good. What does she sound like?'

'Mmm. Youngish, foreign – French, I'd say, but speaks perfect English. Funny, I hadn't thought of him being married – I suppose I was imagining him another Vic Maidment, one of the boys. Oh – when the landlady at the Queen's Head said he wasn't pubbable, perhaps she meant he was terribly domesticated. Wife's probably a cordon bleu.'

81

Rodney was lighter in spirit, thankful for what sounded like a normal contact instead of the master-thief image Doran had been creating. He was not reconciled to her following the trail of the stolen objects, since she had now become more precious to him than he had believed possible, and with Keat's indomitable gipsy in his mind he reflected that his young lady was also as brave as Margaret Queen and bold as Amazon: admirable but dangerous qualities. People who got themselves involved in major thefts were known to finish up at the bottom of rivers or beneath motorways. He said so, and she smiled, not really listening.

'Something occurs to me,' she said. 'We're free for the rest of the day, now we don't have to track down Taddeus. What shall we do?' They exchanged long, thoughtful looks. Doran said, 'Quite right, it would be decadent, on such a beautiful day. Why don't we go back to Stratford? There are lots of things to do besides trailing round the streets. We could walk along the canal path and go round Mary Arden's house and see the treen.'

'Treen?'

'Wooden bygones, things for the dairy and the farm. Rural crafts. Then we could drive across to Charlecote and look at the deer in Sir Thomas Lucy's park, where the Bard *didn't* poach them because there wasn't a deer park in his time. After that we could drive round by Shottery and see Anne's garden and the woods.'

'What woods?'

' "Tell him the woods are green at Shottery, Fuller of flowers than any woods in the world." Clemence Dane. *Will Shakespeare.*'

'My dear girl, I fear things have moved on. When I took my . . . ' He hastily revised the sentence. 'When I went there a few years ago there was no sign of woods, and precious little else that Anne's ghost would recognize if she came back on the trail of her courting days

But if you want to go and look for them we will. Anything you like.'

'What I should like most,' meditated Doran, 'would be to go to the theatre tonight. And don't ask "What theatre?" There's only one in these parts. Well, basically, though it's got two offspring.'

'But I thought you said it had scenery made of packing-cases and actors dressed in paper bags or something – didn't you? Besides, we'd never get in at such short notice.'

'I don't care what the production's like, I just want to go. As for getting in, I feel lucky today. Just you see.'

Rodney saw, and marvelled. After barely a quarter of an hour's queueing, Doran's luck brought them two returned tickets. Their afternoon was as successful as only an unplanned excursion can be. Tourists seemed to melt away at their approach; conversely, the descendants of Sir Thomas's deer were drawn to them, sensing, Rodney said, a certain fawn-like quality in Doran, while Anne's garden bloomed in such fragrant profusion that he was moved to remark that where'er she trod the blushing flowers should rise, and all things flourish where'er she turned her eyes.

The play was *Troilus and Cressida*. Hand in hot hand they sat entranced through that bitter tragi-comedy of war and lust and jealousy, of a passionate boy and a faithless girl. To Rodney it seemed the perfect play for that night. There was something very satisfying in watching a lover's agonies when one was deliriously happy. He remembered that evening – could it have been only last Saturday? – when he had addressed a cat in Doran's lane on the subject of Troilus sighing out his soul on the Grecian walls. He remembered Richenda, a Cressida if ever he saw one, and was deeply thankful for his escape.

They emerged into warm summer dusk. Trees on the Bancroft had blossomed into glowing fruit, electric fairy lights, the river gleamed dark silver. 'Magic,' Doran said. 'More and more magic.'

Much later, in their bed high above the murmur of the little stream, Rodney whispered 'O Cressida, how often have I wished me thus.'

In Stratford during the afternoon Doran had cashed a cheque. After breakfast next morning they drove to Melody Lee's shop. Doran thought it would probably be shut. 'She didn't look like an early riser, but I shall have no compunction about knocking her up. If she answers the door in lovely disarray you'll just have to look elsewhere, like a true gentleman.'

There was a *Closed* sign on the door and no light inside. Repeated bangings brought no answer. They stood back and looked up at windows over which curtains were drawn. 'Well, dammit,' Doran said, 'a bit much when I'd told her we'd be back early this morning. We might be driving to Aberdeen today for all she knows.'

'Perhaps she's hard of hearing.'

'Her hearing was all right yesterday, and she'd have to be stone deaf not to have heard that knocker.'

' "Here's a knocking indeed—" ' began Rodney, then abruptly stopped. In the theatre it was thought extremely unlucky to quote a certain play about a certain Scottish Laird, and the superstition had spread to him. Instead he suggested that they try round the back of the cottage. It had no garden, merely a cinder path that led to a yard full of empty boxes and containers and some plastic sacks of rubbish, none too well secured. 'Phew. I wonder how popular she is with local refuse collectors.' Doran looked up at a small window next to the back door. 'I suppose that's the window of the room she came out of. Can you see into it? I can't reach.'

Rodney stood on an empty box and peered through the dirty pane. At first he could see nothing but a small untidy room, a table and signs of a meal and a beer bottle, a crate with its lid off and fabric spilling out, a pan standing on a miniature cooker.

A splash of colour on the floor caught his eye. It was scarlet cloth. 'An old red blanket cloak she wore.' Beneath it was an outflung foot in a shabby plaid slipper. He did not want to look further, but it was impossible not to follow the scarlet up to the livid open-eyed face, no longer nut brown but a horrible grey on which the gaudy lipstick stood out like a wound. Like the wound beneath it.

Descending from the box he told the waiting Doran, 'Prepare yourself, love. Melody won't be wanting her cash, and we're in trouble.'

CHAPTER SIX

You must be pretty deep to catch weasels asleep . . .

They telephoned the nearest police station, Owlscot, since there was no obvious way of handling the situation themselves. When the police car arrived they were sitting in the Volvo, apprehensive though outwardly calm, and saying little to each other. Rodney wished profoundly that he had not tried to influence Fate by praying for their journey to be diverted, so that Doran would have less time to investigate Tony Taddeus. Doran was excited, interested, sorry for the woman dealer whose fate might well be her own one of these days if she sat in her shop without locking the door. What could be easier for a villain than to slip in and kill a lone woman? It had happened memorably a stone's throw from Charing Cross Station, a shop assistant stabbed to death as she sat knitting. The killer had taken a snuff-box and a case of Edwardian plated spoons. He had never been traced.

The police sergeant who dismounted from the car was altogether more of a regulation model than Thornboro of Honeyford. Large of body, with the face of a very plain longcase clock, he was the archetypal sergeant of fiction, slow to elicit facts, slow to register them. His companion was a young constable who appeared to have got out of bed very recently.

'So,' said Sergeant Davy ponderously, 'the first you

knew of this business was when you looked in through the rear window and saw the deceased?'

'Yes,' Rodney said. 'At least, we . . .'

'You what?'

'Yes. I mean, yes, it was.'

'Very well. Cummins, round the back, and bring the kit with you.'

Doran and Rodney followed. The kit proved to be a canvas hold-all in which were neatly stored hammers, screwdrivers, pliers and other break-in impedimenta. After a glance through the window, to make sure that the story was not a frivolous fabrication, Davy ordered his constable to get to work on the back door. The old wood splintered easily, falling away to make a hole through which Cummins put his arm to draw the bolts. But the bolts had not been used. The door remained tight shut, and the constable, demolishing the entire bottom panel, crawled in.

'Spring lock,' he called from inside. 'I'll let you in at the front.'

Doran whispered to Rodney, 'Whoever killed her simply walked out of the door and slammed it behind him. She probably let him in that way, because the front's well and truly locked. I shook it and it wouldn't move.'

In the small stuffy back room all four looked down at her, a collapsed rag doll. Doran thought she would not have recognized the face for the one she had seen the day before, so complete was the change in it. Rodney had often seen death among his parishioners, had sat by deathbeds or visited the bereaved soon afterwards, but none of the corpses had looked like this one, dead by violence. The neck was slashed, horribly bloody, and a pool of coagulated blood was beneath it on the floor-boards. He wished he had not enjoyed his break-fast so heartily.

Sergeant Davy threw them both a warning look. 'Step back please. Leave that door alone, that's the way the murderer got out. Nothing to be touched. Stand by, Cummins, while I phone.'

They heard his voice in the shop droning on, reporting the 'incident' at length, requesting the presence of a police surgeon, giving times, details and road identifications. Returning, he stated baldly that he would require the witnesses (or suspects, as by now they were sure he thought them) to accompany him to the police station. Doran, feeling that it had all happened before, pointed out that she could hardly leave her car standing in the lane on a yellow line. The problem seemed not to have struck Davy, nor a solution.

'I could follow your car,' she suggested.

'Not without an escort, miss.'

'Oh. Well, your constable could come with me, and you could take my . . . Mr Barham.'

This arrangement, though obviously revolutionary, was at length agreed. Rodney shot her a wild look and was driven away in the passenger seat of the police car, while the young constable sat beside her, yawning at frequent intervals. She was too perturbed to make conversation with him.

Instinct told her that this experience of the nick was going to be less pleasant than the last one, an intuition confirmed when the car in front of her drew up at a remarkably ugly police station which could have doubled as the local jail, and possibly did.

Sam Eastry, community policeman of Abbotsbourne, was checking his Honda in the garden of the police house, about to set off for the scene of a brawl outside a pub a few miles away. A gang of youths who had been drinking all night had besieged the door well before opening time, and were throwing bottles through the windows, as well as attacking everybody in sight. His HQ at Eastgate was calling in extra constabulary to deal with the affray.

He was about to mount his bike when his wife Lydia called from the front door. 'Telephone for you!'

Sam looked at his watch. 'Who is it? I ought to be half-way there by now.'

'Owlscot. West Midlands.'

Sam swore. It never rained but it poured, and he had had two hectic days. 'Constable Eastry,' he told the telephone crisply.

'Ah,' said a precise voice. 'Inspector Fearnlie, Owlscot, Evesham Division. Good morning. I'd like a word with you, Constable, about a lady we have here from your area. A Miss Dora Ann Fairweather, she tells us.'

Sam thought frantically. He had not even known that Doran had gone away. Yet there she was, in the West Midlands, apparently in some sort of trouble. It was no new thing. He had a warm, avuncular relationship with her, at once protective and admiring, and had seen her through some dangerous moments in last year's Abbotsbourne crimes. Not an intellectual, Sam yet prided himself on his knowledge of the exploits of Sherlock Holmes, in the lore of which he found Doran a more than worthy game-player. Sam had no detective ambitions, but feared that Doran had, and that in real life they were dangerous things for a young lady to harbour.

'Yes,' he said carefully. 'Miss Fairweather's a neighbour of mine. A friend, you might say.'

'Good.' The prim voice sounded cheered. 'And no doubt you know Mr Barham.'

Sam's mind blanked. Mr Barham? Who the devil was Mr Barham?

'Ah. Mr Barham,' he said, praying for an inspiration that would enable him not to let Doran down. 'Let me see. That would be the Mr Barham who . . . '

'You must know Mr Barham, Constable,' reproved the voice, 'as I'm told he shares Miss Fairweather's home.'

'Of course, of course.' Sam wished that he could suddenly de-materialize and be somewhere else, not taking part in this present conversation. At the other end he could hear Doran's voice and the inspector's; then Fearnlie came back to him.

'Miss Fairweather would like a word with you.'

'Sam, hello.' At least she sounded bright and cheerful. A shade too bright? And gabbling. 'I don't suppose you knew Richard's other name was Barham, did you, as he's only been staying with me for the last day or two. You've heard me talk about him a lot, of course. We decided quite suddenly to drive up here for a holiday. Quite a Scandal in Bohemia, as you might say. At least,' and she laughed lightly, falsely, 'not really scandalous, but it reminds me a lot of that episode when Holmes got himself into Irene's house – only *in reverse,* as it were. Don't you think so?' Understand, understand, crack the code, she was silently telling him, and he thought feverishly. In the case of *A Scandal in Bohemia* Holmes had disguised himself as an elderly clergyman in order to gain admission into the adventuress's villa. An elderly clergyman in reverse . . . He understood.

'Of course, Doran, I know who you mean, I just didn't connect the name at first. Now what are you two up to – not been arrested, I hope?'

'Oh no, nothing like that. It's just that I got on the track of an antiques theft and I'm afraid it's led to a murder and Rod – Richard and I came across the body. The Inspector's just checking that we're clean – isn't that the right expression?'

'If you say so, Doran. Can I have another word with him? He spoke briefly and reassuringly of Doran's character, profession, and status in Abbotsbourne, and added that so far as he knew her friend Mr Barham was a highly respected person. He hoped the Owlscot police would soon get whoever was responsible for the murder, and wished them luck.

He turned away from the telephone wiping sweat

91

from his brow. Lydia had been listening to the conversation, fascinated; the perfect police wife, she knew that he would tell her about it if discretion allowed – if not, not.

Discretion did allow, since the matter was a domestic one, on his own patch, to all intents and purposes.

'Where's the vicar?' he said.

Surprised, Lydia answered, 'Gone away, Vi told me, but she doesn't know where, just that he said he was off for a holiday and Mrs Oliphant asked Vi to do out his room.'

'*I* see. Well, I find it hard to believe, but he's up there with Doran, calling himself Richard Barham, for some reason.'

'Barham? What on earth for? I expect it's some joke of theirs. Do you mean that they . . . ? After all this time?'

Husband and wife exchanged a meaning look. Both knew very well of the deep attachment between Doran and Rodney, so long frustrated, though it was something they did not discuss with each other or anybody else. The village grapevine, Vi, would hear nothing from Lydia.

'Well,' Lydia said, 'good for them, poor things. That daughter of his ought to be in a home, if you ask me, though if our Jane had lived and gone the same way I expect we'd have felt like the vicar does.' Jane had been lost to them at nine years old, the victim of a giant transport that had skidded off the road on to the pavement. They had their bright son Ben for comfort, but daughters were special.

'I expect so. Well, Doran's run into something nasty up there, just as you might expect. At least it's not her that's got murdered.'

'Murdered?'

'I'll tell you when I get back, not that I know much myself.' Sam kissed her swiftly. 'Those lads'll have the place afire by now, I shouldn't wonder.'

Lydia watched the Honda roar off. Her romantic heart rejoiced at Sam's news. Two nice young people, who'd kept themselves respectably apart for so long, not at all the way so many went on nowadays, running away together at last. It was really very like *Romeo and Juliet*, the film of which she and Sam had seen on their honeymoon. Only that story had ended badly, and she hoped young Doran's romance would not.

Murder, indeed: they had seen enough of that last year.

Inspector Fearnlie contemplated the two witnesses who sat opposite him. The girl had gone a bright, betraying pink during her telephone conversation with Constable Eastry; there had been lies in it somewhere, and a false name, and a lot of gabble which had been some sort of code. He had checked, out of her hearing, with the Honeyford police, to whom she had not stated that Mr Barham shared her house, and Constable Eastry had obviously never heard of the man. The inspector's gaze dwelt on the small cross Mr Barham wore round his neck, fully revealed by the open shirt. It was indeed small, but not the kind of cheap symbol young men often wore: he would describe it as more of a crucifix, well made and probably worth quite a bit. And there was something about Mr Barham's voice, very clear, very educated and with a carrying quality. He could, of course, be an actor – there were plenty around, so near Stratford. But Inspector Fearnlie thought not. He guessed, correctly, Mr Barham's calling. If Rodney had suddenly burst into a heartfelt rendering of *Salve Regina,* Fearnlie would not have been surprised. But he had got one thing wrong: the denomination. A Roman Catholic priest on holiday with a young woman: of course there'd be a false name, and lies and blushes.

Briskly he summed up his inquiries. 'So the object,

the piece of pottery you bought from Mrs Lee, wasn't in her shop when we found the body?'

'No,' Doran said.

'But you'd know it again?'

'Anywhere. I should think the person who stole it from Lady Timberlake has got it back.' Fond of docketing people as antique objects, she had Fearnlie down as a china greyhound, one of those gaudily coloured red and white, which used to decorate so many cottage mantel-pieces, dead hares in their mouths. Rockingham, usually, or Staffs. Sharp-nosed, sharp-eyed, sharp-eared. Even more like a weasel, perhaps. You could probably buy porcelain weasels nowadays, with so many artists modelling creatures of the wild . . . 'I beg your pardon?' She realized the inspector was addressing her.

'You'll let us know where we can contact you, while you're in this part of the world? Now I have your present address, the Leaping Trout, Aldersley. And the telephone number. If you *should* happen to hear of this missing object, or any of the others, we'd be most obliged to know of it. But I'd keep clear of suspicious characters, if I were you. We'll give you ring in a day or two, just to check.'

Hopefully, they moved forward in their chairs, but he went on smoothly, a surgeon who had just found another suspicious area of tissue: 'I'd like to run you out to Honeyford House and have a word with Lady Timberlake. She may have some more ideas about the robberies by now. It'll only take a quarter of an hour.'

There was nothing they could do to resist the sugges-tion: or request or command, whichever way you looked at it. They had answered endless questions, they had signed statements, Doran had avoided specific mention of the clock until she felt that CLOCK was written on her forehead with letters of fire. They had drunk several cups of lukewarm tea in thick cups (but it would have been unreasonable to expect Worcester or Coalport) and eaten sandwiches brought from a pub by a young constable who was still at the tea-boy stage of officialdom.

They had, in fact, been reasonably and kindly treated, without a hint of bullying, by this shrewd sandy man who had a photograph of a pretty wife and two strapping children on his desk. They were nevertheless exhausted, drained: and now Lady Timberlake.

The door of Honeyford House was open, as before. They went in, and Fearnlie called loudly on the ground floor, before exploring the kitchen regions. A mountain of dirty crockery loomed over the sink and on the table a plate of what had perhaps been scrambled egg had solidified to the consistency of plaster food in a doll's house. Rodney averted his eyes.

'I just hope she isn't lying dead somewhere,' he murmured to Doran, who murmured back, 'No such luck.' Indeed, when they returned to the hall Lady Timberlake was descending the stairs, haltingly, clinging to one banister. An aroma of spirits descended with her.

Inspector Fearnlie introduced himself, apologized for the intrusion, cautioned her against leaving the door unlocked, all in one efficient sentence. 'Perhaps you remember Miss Fairweather and Mr Barham – they came to see the house the other day and Miss Fairweather pointed out to you that several items had been removed from your collection. Now—'

The old lady backed away dramatically, pointing. 'I know who they are! Don't you tell me Miss This and Mr That, because I won't have it.'

Fearnlie's eyes were bright with hopeful interest. 'Really, Lady Timberlake? Perhaps you'd tell me anything you may know.'

She trembled, shaking her stick in the air. 'Bonnie and Clyde, that's who they are! *I* know, I saw the film – they can't deceive me. Well-known bank robbers, that's who, and they've taken all my pretty things. You'll find they've got guns on them. Look for the guns, look for the guns, or we'll all be shot!' She began to utter short sharp shrieks. Fearnlie gestured with his head at the two alleged criminals, who unobtrusively removed themselves.

When he joined them in the garden he wore a rueful, totally unofficial smile.

'Sorry about that. I'd heard she'd gone a bit . . . as you see, but I didn't know it was as far as that. Never mind. I hope she didn't upset you, Miss Fairweather.'

'Not unduly. She said much the same sort of thing when we were here before. Inspector – you don't suppose she's mad enough to have hidden the things herself?'

'That had just occurred to me; very sharp of you, Miss Fairweather. I'll get a search warrant and we'll have a tactful look around, tomorrow, perhaps. I think I'll get a spring lock put on that front door . . .'

Doran was not feeling as sharp as he had said. She recalled that there was one item Lady Timberlake could not possibly have hidden away. Two, come to think of it. Where, she wondered, was the pillion piece now?

They were back at the Trout, eating a huge tea in the garden, with scones, cream and jam.

'I don't know what police tea's made of,' Rodney ruminated. 'The contents of their vacuum cleaner? Dottles from earnest coppers' pipes? Grocers' fire salvage? This is a different beverage.'

'If they ring here,' Doran said gloomily,' they'll ask for Miss Fairweather, and be told she doesn't exist. Then that weasely inspector will ask for Mrs Barham – I saw him, weighing us up, me and my ring and you and your cross – and the whole thing will be out.'

'Does it matter? Sticks and stones may break my bones, you know. Anyway, Inspector Fearnlie's not there as official guardian of public morals – at least he is, of course, but not of private ones. I should think he's seen it all in his time, and who worries, nowadays?' Except me, he thought.

'Well, I still don't fancy the idea. I think we ought to move on, out of their catchment area.'

'And preferably out of the catchment area of who-ever did in Melody Lee. You remember what he said about that?'

'The exterior jugular neatly severed by a very sharp instrument and a hand that knew what it was doing. Horrible. He shouldn't have let that out to us, but he did it to scare us off. The poor old thing: not that she was even very old. You know what I think? I think she wormed that Whieldon pillion piece out of whoever stole it, and then just couldn't resist putting it into her stock. Somehow the Whoever found out, and did her in, and nicked it back.'

Rodney was silent. Violence sickened him more than it did the fiction-fed Doran. He was torn between a strong urge to linger in their vulnerable Paradise, their first place together, and an equally strong one to remove Doran as far from danger as possible. She countered any decision he might have made by saying, 'Well, we'll have to stay here until after tonight – we're eating with the Taddeuses, or Taddeii.'

'Oh. I'd forgotten, with all this helping the police with their inquiries. Must we?'

'If he's back from wherever he's been, yes. She said she'd let us know about six.'

Rodney sighed. He had been looking forward to a peaceful dinner in the Trout's secluded dining alcove, with nobody asking him any questions. 'Who are we supposed to be, then? It's getting confusing, you popping in and out of Mrs Barham's identity.'

'Well, I've got to be me, because of the Maidment connection - and I'm afraid you're stuck with Mr Barham. At least the police didn't put two and two together with his name – perhaps they didn't recognize it.'

'Recognize it? My darling dreamer, they wouldn't have recognized it if we'd said that he – I – wrote the *Ingoldsby Legends,* because they've never heard of him, or them. They wouldn't have recognized it if I'd said my name was Alfred Lord Tennyson, Robert Browning, or Henry Wadsworth Longfellow. People don't read the poets any more.'

'You ought to write, you know; you're wasting your time on sermons. No, I don't mean to be insulting, your sermons aren't half bad. But why don't you do an anthology? Perhaps of all the surprising bits of poetry that people don't know and ought to. You'd be awfully good at it.'

'Yes, I should, shouldn't I. Perhaps I will. Meanwhile I suggest that we go in and have very long baths.'

'Baths,' Doran repeated thoughtfully. 'There *is* a shower room.'

Rodney looked blank. 'You mean you want our bath and I can have a shower?'

'Not quite. You *are* sweet, you know. Come upstairs and I'll show you. Then we'll go down to the bar and have a stiff drink.'

As they went upstairs, entwined, to the interest of the chambermaid, Rodney asked, 'Did you know that Barham was very fond of gin? He called it Ginnums.'

'The Ginnums we shall have, at six sharp. After the shower.'

They sat at a small, chic table in the small, chic restaurant that was Nina's Bistro. It seemed not to fit at all its setting, a tiny Cotswold village, being notably smart in a Londonish way with mock-ups of Victorian gas-lamps, prints of the lesser-known Impressionists, framed covers of *Vogue,* and a great deal of almost unhealthily healthy greenery.

Nina herself was not visible, being the chef. Their waiter was known as Albert, though his non-localized accent and appearance suggested that he might have been called almost anything, from Mick to Baldassare. The Taddeii addressed him often; they were obviously favoured clients. Only one other couple was dining, since the hour was early. Doran had asked by telephone if they might meet not too late, as they had had a tiring day.

Doran was just a shade relieved by the Taddeii's own appearance. (She could not bring herself to think of them as Taddeuses.) Tony Taddeus was on the large side – a man who enjoyed food – fortyish, or a little more, his balding scalp fringed with dark curling hair, his complexion dark, florid with rich living, she guessed. It was easy to see that his origins were probably Greek, and equally easy to deduce the reason for his being popularly known as Tony rather than Antoniou. His smile was frequent and infectious, his voice mellifluous. He seemed an improvement on anything Eastgate had in the way of dealers.

Cecile Taddeus might have been tailored to provide a matching contrast to her husband. Where he was plump, she was slim. Against his darkness, she was of a clear pale complexion with light brown hair, very short and immaculately cut. In age, she might have been a little younger than Tony, or much younger, or the same age: who knows how old Mona Lisa Gioconda was when Leonardo painted her? Cecile's features were good – regular, straight nose, small mouth, grey-blue eyes. She was not beautiful, or even pretty – just comely, Doran thought. Sometimes likenesses were elusive, but in Cecile's case an instant comparison flashed into Doran's mind, the portrait of a young woman by one of the Cranachs, a calm oval face below a flat Tudor bonnet with a jewelled net hiding the hair. The very faintest of French accents tinged Cecile's soft voice. She smelt expensive. *Femme,* Doran guessed.

Tony talked shop with Doran, while Cecile put in occasional intelligent remarks and Rodney, who was tired and hungry, applied himself to his food. Yes, said Tony, Vic Maidment had been in those parts recently and they had met.

'Curious sort of chap – not exactly giving, is he?'

'Not at all. Quite the reverse.'

'Anyway, he found quite a bit up here, I gathered. And no, I don't know your friend Howell Evans, and Maidment didn't mention him. The fact is, I haven't been down your way for much too long, certainly not since – when did you open your shop? No, definitely not since then. I ought to make more time, I know, but what with my restoration work and keeping up with the local sales I seem to be on a non-stop roundabout – *La Ronde,* in fact, only less amusing.'

'You're lucky to keep busy with local sales,' Doran said.

'My dear, we have an astonishing number. Don't know what it is, possibly the cold round here in winter, killing the old people off – or perhaps it's just inflation and the influx of weekenders rather than residents.'

'They're lovely, the sales,' Cecile said. 'I go to them all. I buy things because I can't resist them, and so my house is always changing round because I keep them – don't I, Tony?'

'Too often.'

'I am so lucky to have two places, where I can decorate in different styles. I can go to the flat when it is not let and entertain myself. But I like the *rocaille,* the rococo, best, and the Louis Quinze. The other week I buy – bought – a most beautiful *vase de nuit,* eighteenth-century all covered in flowers. Tony said it had a prettier French name, didn't you, darling? *Bourdalou,* that was it. And before that I found – what do you think? – an art nouveau bidet, all butterflies.'

'Doran will think you have very limited and rather low tastes,' said Tony. 'She does buy other things, I assure you, Doran, quite unconnected with bathrooms.'

Rodney murmured, as much to himself as to

100

them,' "Cloacina, goddess of the tide, Whose sable streams beneath the city glide . . ." '

'Pardon?' asked Cecile prettily.

'Mr Gay on Sewers,' Rodney interpreted. 'Sorry, I ramble sometimes.' He returned to his wild cherry soup and the exquisite Sancerre, perfectly chilled, for which Tony had rejected Albert's suggestion of the house white. Rodney guessed that this was a standing custom.

The soup plates departed, to be replaced by sole stuffed with mushroom and anchovy. Tony assured them that Nina's fish was invariably fresh, though Doran wondered how this could be, since they were in the centre of England. She decided to come to the reason for the meeting, asking Tony whether he had a shop.

'Not an actual shop. I'm a dealer's dealer, and a restorer. But chums are always welcome to look in, if I know they're coming. I do a tremendous lot of postal trade, so I'm not too keen on interruptions. We're all in one, home and business premises, a big Georgian house with stacks of room in it. We have this flat, too, which we let to friends, as Cecile told you.' He shot a look at his wife which Doran fancied was not altogether cordial. Perhaps he had a tax fiddle going, and she was not supposed to mention the flat. 'We may even get more room, if the church affair comes round the way we want it.'

'What church affair?' Rodney asked.

'The village – Lippett Green – has a small church, St Faith's, been disused for half a century now – it's in a poor state, floorboards rotten and most of the windows broken by louts. The council want to pull it down – they would, wouldn't they – and build houses, but the other proposition is that it should be made into an antiques supermarket, or hypermarket or whatever. Now that appeals to me. It would bring trade in, attract dealers from further off, and generally liven things up, providing we keep control of the sort of stuff that's sold – no stinking second-hand clothes, for instance.'

'Has it been deconsecrated?'

Taddeus glanced curiously at Rodney. 'I suppose so. I really don't know when. Anyway, it's a good site. I wouldn't mind putting money into it.'

'There would be stalls with nice things,' said Cecile. 'I would not have to go far from home to buy, but Tony would lock me in, I think.'

'That's right. You're the original magpie, my girl, that's what you are.' He gave her ear a playful tweak, at which she squealed sharply. Rodney found himself about to quote some apt lines from *The Jackdaw of Rheims,* about jewellery and a predatory bird, but stopped himself in time.

Doran had been waiting for an opportunity to come to the point.

'I wonder if . . . have you heard of Lady Timberlake?'

'Widow of the Camden Town guy. Yes, heard of, never seen.'

'We have. Been to see her. It's a strange story, and it's really why I wanted to meet you and ask your advice.' She embarked on the tale of the robberies (leaving out mention of the clock), the discovery of the pillion piece and the murder of Melody Lee. 'That's why I said we'd had a tiring day, you see. I'd like to know what you think of it all.'

Taddeus did not answer immediately. The very faintest of changes came over his florid face; Doran's antennae quivered. She had given him some kind of shock, or at least surprise. That, or his moral sense was outraged at the news that a poor old lady had been robbed. It seemed unlikely.

Cecile had been listening raptly. 'But we know Melody Lee! A very dirty lady who sells rubbish. She has a stall at the Rother Market at Stratford on Fridays.'

'Correction, had,' Tony said. 'What a nasty way to go. Poor old cow. Well, well . . .'

'The stalls are very assorted,' Cecile said, 'everything from rubbish, tat and very cheap nasty clothes to quite good things – it's a matter of luck, and parking, of course. I found one or two things on Melody's, quite a nice Mary Gregory beaker which I don't think she knew was right, and a pretty valentine, a couple going up in the air in a lace-trimmed balloon wearing such bright smiles and a lot more lace . . . '

Doran became impervious to the description, wondering how one could be bothered about details of Bohemian glass and valentines when a dealer one knew had just been murdered. Cecile had seemed so carried away by the Rother Market stalls that her accent had melted away, possibly helped by the Sancerre. Wonderful, how wine loosened the tongue in a strange language. She recalled spending three days all but dumb in Normandy before an unusual indulgence in the wine of the region followed by Calvados had brought on an embarrassing burst of French fluency.

She was studying Cecile's earrings, tiny swinging baubles with garnet centres, set in paste imitating diamonds. They were an unusual shape. And she had seen them before, displayed in a case on white velvet, with other early jewellery. They were the sort of ornaments she liked wearing, and accordingly noticed. They had belonged to a Victorian lady of Honeyford House.

Absorbed in this discovery, she failed to see that Rodney had changed colour and appeared distressed.

Rodney realized quite suddenly that the restaurant was spinning round him in an alarming manner. A combination of tiredness, nervous strain, rich food, Sancerre, a lot of unaccustomed lovemaking and possibly the Trout's strong double Ginnums had conspired with the mention of Melody Lee's corpse to turn him dizzy and faint. Afraid of being sick on the spot, he said hastily, 'Would you excuse me? Feeling a bit odd, need some fresh air.'

The toilet signs were clear, avoiding such Stratfordian coynesses as Knaves and Wenches or Codpieces and Farthingales. But he passed by them into the small patio at the back of the restaurant, where laid tables stood among tubs and pots of flowers. There he sat on a rustic bench and put his head down until the spinning sensation began to recede.

He was not, after all, going to disgrace himself by being sick, but the thought of more food and wine was loathsome to him. He longed for peace, silence, and Doran to himself. He allowed himself ten minutes in the balmy evening air, with closed eyes. The strains of taped Vivaldi floated out through an open window. Curious, how they only seemed to have heard of Vivaldi, among all the composers there were. Purcell. Why not Purcell? Elgar? A bit strong, perhaps. Vaughan Williams? Local colour, V.W. Like trueborn Cotswold men, brave boys, like trueborn Cotswold men . . .

A hand was on his shoulder, a soft voice at his ear.

'Rodney. Wake up, time to go. Are you all right?'

Back in the restaurant concern was expressed, advice given. The men shook hands, Cecile planted two light kisses on Doran's cheeks, saying that she would cook for them next time, *chez nous*. Nina emerged from the back regions and was ceremoniously introduced, a little creature almost lost behind a plastic pinafore.

At last they were out of the place, alone, in the Volvo, with Doran at the wheel. As she started the engine Rodney said, 'Just a minute. Please can we not talk about that meal? I'm alright, not ill or anything, but I think I've drunk too much and I just want to be quiet.'

Doran nodded. Very carefully and at a low speed she drove back the seven miles to their inn. One thing they didn't need was another encounter with the police.

As they were preparing for bed Rodney asked, 'Did you get any helpful tips out of Taddeus while I was outside giving my famous impression of a sick parrot?'

'Nothing definite, but general optimism.' Doran

hoped her casual tone would not betray the suspicions that had begun to grow in her mind. 'He's been around quite a bit before he settled in his own place. Porcelain's his line, and what he doesn't know about faking it isn't worth knowing. There was a man he met in Wolverhampton used to turn out Dresden, proper marks and all to impress the punters, and another's rolling Staffs. off the conveyor belt that would take in Ralph Wood if he'd lived to see it.'

'So? What about Honeyford House?'

'He's going to make discreet inquiries and look round a bit. We shan't hear anything for the moment. I told him I thought Maidment was worth a look or two, and I only hope it doesn't lead to the clock.' It was hard to have to deceive her love, but she knew what he would say.

She stood at the window, looking out over the garden milky with starlight. 'Aldebaran,' she said to the night. 'Vega, Sirius, Antares. Capella, Algol, Lyra. Castor, Betelguese, Orion.'

Rodney stood behind her, his hands cupping her breasts. 'You can't see all those, surely.'

'Possibly not. I just like their names. "Look at all the fire-folk sitting in the air . . . " Do you think we ought to move on tomorrow?'

'Yes, if Taddeus hasn't any immediate news. Let's go over the border to Somerset and see the Mendips, and the Bishop's swans at Wells, ringing the bell for their dinner.'

'And Glastonbury and Guinevere's tomb.'

'And, now I recollect,' said Rodney, 'a dear little church whose name escapes me, where only the font's survived from the past, and one of the new bells informs one that "Our merry peal is mainly due To Mr and Mrs Gerald Carew."'

Doran laughed. 'How Sam Eastry would love that, him and his precious bells. I hope the Oliphants don't mind all that evening practice. So we go to Somerset tomorrow.'

'Meanwhile,' his lips were urgent on her throat, his arms warm and close round her, 'let's have one other gaudy night.'

It was not until morning that Rodney remembered guiltily that he had forgotten to make his routine evening call to Arline and Helena. Ah, well. They had the telephone number of the Trout – if anything were wrong he would have heard. After a memorable breakfast he reluctantly paid the bill, feeling as though he were signing away something precious.

In the early morning air it seemed a crime to get in the car and drive, shut away from it. Rodney said that he wanted to walk to Kingsleach, two miles or so away, and look at a remarkable wall-painting of the Harrowing of Hell.

'You do that,' Doran said, 'assuming you can get into the church.'

'I will – I always do. Coming with me?'

'No, I don't think I will. I have a terrific urge to walk to the top of the hill again. Tell you what – I'll have my walk, and then pick you up here in the car, shall I? An hour – hour and a half?'

Faintly disappointed, Rodney agreed; he had wanted to see the last of Paradise with her. They put their luggage in the car boot, locked it, and set off in opposite directions. Doran let him get out of sight before running back to the car.

The Harrowing of Hell proved to be all the guide-book said it was, its vivid colours lately retrieved after five and a half centuries under the whitewash slapped on it by the Reformation. Rodney made a sketch of the writhing serpent under the Holy foot, the Cross sustaining a clutch of rescued souls. He then found some very curious corbels and a late Victorian window which made him laugh loudly in a church fortunately empty but for him. Beside a sickbed a well-wisher was informing the patient, presumably moribund, that 'The Master is come and calleth for thee', indicating the sacred figure hovering outside the door. The sufferer's expression of unrestrained annoyance prompted Rodney to sit down and rough out a number of mildly irreverent captions to show Doran later. ('Oh, blast! I wanted to watch *Dallas* . . .')

The walk back to the Trout was slightly uphill; towards the end of it he hurried, seeing that more than an hour and a half had passed.

But the Volvo was not standing in the inn's car park, where he had left it. Mrs Wilford, surprised, said that she had not seen Mrs Barham drive off, and she had certainly not come back inside. He checked their room, which was exactly as when he had last seen it.

Rodney went asking up and down in the tiny village. But nobody had seen a blue Volvo hatchback pass, in either direction. He returned to the Trout, where Mrs Wilford took pity on his distracted expression, and brought him a cup of coffee.

'You sit here on the bench and cool down. She's thought of something and gone off to get it, you'll see. Maybe gone into Chipping. Just take it easy, Mr Barham.'

Several times she glanced out of the bar window. An hour passed. Still Rodney sat there, or paced up and down, his face drawn into ageing lines of worry.

At half past twelve he entered the cool bar and went through it to the hall pay phone.

To the desk sergeant at Owlscot police station he said, 'May I speak to Inspector Fearnlie, please?'

CHAPTER SEVEN

And where doth tarry Nelly Cook, that staid and
comely lass?

Ay, where?

Inspector Fearnlie had been having a dull morning. Youths had smashed a shop window overnight and there had been an hysterical complaint about a rogue cat which had savaged the neighbour's hens and breakfasted on a carp from his pond. It was not enough to keep an active man going.

He was all the more interested and stimulated to receive Rodney's call. If he had been in the habit of compiling a case book, this would have gone down in it as the Return of the Renegade Priest. He listened patiently, sympathetically.

'So you last saw Miss Fairweather just after nine o'clock this morning, sir. And you've no idea where she might be?'

'Not the slightest. It's so unlike her – she'd have left me a note, a message, anything. She's very thoughtful about things like that.'

'And you'd had no sort of disagreement, sir? A few words, an argument, anything that might make a lady feel – well, like going off on her own to cool down a bit?'

'No. Nothing. Quite the reverse.' Rodney was remembering the last few minutes in the bedroom he would never forget as long as he lived. The old house had been quiet and they had heard the little stream talking, as it had talked at night. He had said, 'Will you marry me, when we get home – if everything's still all right? Arline will cope, and we'll cope somehow, won't we?'

'Yes, I will. Marry you, I mean. It's been fun pretending, but I want the real thing more than anything in the world.' She had kissed him, a very solemnly-betrothed sort of kiss. He had said, rather shakily, ' "As my lady of Suffolk saith, God is a marvellous man." '

'Well, now.' Fearnlie, his theory of a lovers' quarrel demolished, was thinking hard. 'Could Miss Fairweather have gone to someone's help? Driven someone to a hospital after an accident, perhaps? I'll phone round and see if there's any reports. Or – she could have had trouble with the car, and gone off to a garage for repairs. I'll check that, too. Meanwhile, perhaps you could let me have details, sir. The lady's clothing, any distinguishing marks, car number and description – that sort of thing.'

Rodney struggled to remember such details, having a poor head for numbers of any kind and only the vaguest notion of Doran's height and what clothes she had been wearing. He returned to the bar and slumped in a window-seat. Others had come in and were eating and drinking, ignoring him. He had sat, unseeing, for some time, when he was conscious of a presence beside him: the proprietress, Jane Wilford.

In his previous state of euphoria he had hardly been conscious of her except as someone friendly and in keeping with the inn's character. She was regarding him with infinite sympathy in her eyes, which, now he noticed, were blue and pretty, with more lines round them than her age warranted: she was probably younger than he was.

'Sorry to intrude,' she said. 'Couldn't help overhearing part of that – and after what you said. Mrs Barham's not come back, then?'

'No. The police are asking questions – hospitals, and all that. They're being very good.'

'And you hadn't had any trouble – a bit of a tiff?'

'No!' Rodney felt he was shouting. 'We were very happy indeed – except about leaving here. There was nothing wrong at all. I can't understand it. I don't know what to do.'

A soft little hand rested on his. 'You poor dear. I didn't really think there'd been any trouble. You seemed so happy. Anyone could see it, we all could. Betty said, "Just married, you can tell." That's true, isn't it?'

Rodney turned his head away, hoping she would take the gesture for an affirmative, unable to lie outright. 'Yes, I knew it,' Mrs Wilford said. 'I remember what it was like. My James and I were just the same, at first. I thought it would never be any different – but it was.' The blue eyes were swimming in tears. 'Now he's left me, and I can't believe it ever happened, any of it.'

Rodney listened numbly as she told him of her husband's gradual enslavement by a barmaid at another inn, and his sudden cowardly flight, leaving her to run the place and pay off debts. 'It just wasn't like him, not my James at all. If I'd known it was going to happen I think I'd have killed her first. People understand, and they've been very kind and helpful, but it's not the same, when there've been two of you and you're left on your own. So you see, dear, you may have been spared something, if the worst comes to the worst.'

Rodney stared at her, feeling a chill down his spine. 'The worst?'

'I mean if she's had some sort of accident – gone off the road, over the quarry, or crashed into another car. You'll never know anything worse than what you've had, then.'

Rodney went paper-white and put his head in his hands. Mrs Wilford, after a frightened glance, went off hurriedly and returned with a brandy. 'Drink this, Mr

111

Barham. I'm sorry, I shouldn't have said what I did. I'm sure it's nothing like that.'

He drank it off at one draught. 'Thank you . . . I'm all right now. I know I checked out this morning, but in the circumstances I'd like to stay on, if I can, please. Not . . . perhaps not the same room, just a single, if you have one.' To sleep again in that memoried room, without Doran, was something he could not face; and an icy intuition told him she would not be coming back to their room.

Mrs Wilford assured him that it would be all right. There was a small single on the second floor which she would see to at once. He watched her at the far end of the bar, at the little reception desk, and Betty the chef and Vicky the waitress converging on her, all talking about him and his interesting situation. And, because habit takes no account of anxiety or anguish, into his mind popped a pantomime imp with the grisly pantomime legend of the Mistletoe Bough.

> . . .*when Lovell appeared, the children cried*
> *'See! the old man weeps for his fairy bride.'*

Irresistible not to go on with it. 'A skeleton form lay mould'ring there, in the bridal wreath of a lady fair.' He recalled how he had warned her – or himself? – that people who got too deep into crime investigation had been known to finish up at the bottoms of rivers or underneath motorways. At which an attack of the horrors such as he had never known came over him. He strode out of the inn, up the lane, down a wynd and into a farmyard. The farmer's wife could supply him with free-range eggs, cream and late-crop strawberries, but not with information about a girl in a blue Volvo.

Nor could anyone he met, in the village and beyond it, including an ancient man in a bathchair, sunning himself outside his cottage with a tabby cat on his knees, or a young mother with twins in a double pram, or a man on a bicycle who was clearly half-witted. Soon he had run out of people and was walking aimlessly, going always upwards, glad of the effort, of the sun's heat on his head and the tiredness of his feet in light sandals: his Old Testament sandals, Doran had called them.

He reached a height crossed by a limestone wall, and perched on a five-barred gate. Before him spread the Vale of Evesham, a vast plain of sheep-meadow, woodland, orchards rich in ripening fruit, churches and scattered small villages. He wondered where in all those miles his lost girl could be. If she was there at all. He would not let himself think of other possibilities. Away to the north-west was a higher elevation than the one he had climbed: Bredon Hill, which Doran had pointed out to him through the dusk. From a distant church the hour struck, clear in the clear air. *O peal upon our wedding, and we will hear the chime. And come to church in time.*

Four o'clock. Mad, to be rambling so far away from the inn, when a message might have come through. He began to hurry downwards, once stumbling and turning his ankle painfully. By the time he reached the Trout his limbs were jarred with haste, one foot blistered. The front door was locked – impatiently he hurried round to the side, and found Jane Wilford in her private sitting room.

'No, I'm sorry, no message for you. A few odd calls, but nothing about your wife. Where on earth have you been? You look all in.'

'Walking,' he said dully.

'Good gracious, you must have been miles. And you're limping. Sit down and I'll get you some tea. In here – no need to go. Put your feet up on that stool.'

The tea was refreshing. Tactfully she left him alone to drink it, coming back when she judged he would have got over the first shock of disappointment. He had been thinking. What should he do, what action could

113

he take? His mind was clearing – of course, he must ring two numbers; first, the police again. He went to the pay phone in the hall, knowing that Jane Wilford would not be able to help overhearing if he used her own telephone.

Fearnlie said, 'No, I'm sorry, sir. No news at all. We've put out a general call, and of course we'll contact you when we hear anything. One thing I forgot to ask you this morning – is Miss Fairweather subject to any abnormalities? Blackouts, loss of memory, fainting attacks, anything like that?'

Rodney, by now feeling a likely subject himself for all these ailments, said that she was not. The inspector sighed. 'Well, it seemed a chance. Still at the same number, sir? Don't worry, we'll keep in touch with you.'

Don't worry! Rodney laughed hollowly as he hung up. He dialled again, this time Tony Taddeus's number. Cecile answered.

'You again! How nice. Are you well? We were a bit worried about you last night. Did you like Nina's, though?'

'Very nice. Is Tony about?'

'Sure, I'll get him. Tony!'

Taddeus came on the line, a big jolly baritone voice after his wife's trill. 'Well, hello. Good to talk to you again. Better, are you? And how's that delicious Doran?'

'That's why I'm calling you. Tony, has she been to see you?'

'Been to – ? No. Why, did she say she was coming here?'

'No. But you said last night that friends were welcome to visit you at the shop, and I wondered . . . You see, she's disappeared.'

'She's *what?*'

Rodney embarked on the story. 'Nothings been heard of her, the police don't know anything, she's just gone, vanished without trace. And as you're the only

114

people she's met round here I wondered if she'd dashed off to see you, on an impulse. I should have rung you before, but I'm too fraught to think straight. This Honeyford business has been on her mind and I thought perhaps she wanted to talk to you about it.'

'Good God! No, she certainly hasn't been here. What a bloody headache for you.'

'It's that, all right. I wondered – you said you'd make some inquiries about anyone who might know anything about the Honeyford thefts – did you, by any chance?'

A silence. 'Well. I don't like to mention colleagues' names – I mean, we're all in it together, in the Trade, so to speak, and dog doesn't eat dog, but I did just have one thought. There's a man has a shop on the far side of Stratford. Bit of a dodger. Shouldn't have thought he'd have had the remotest interest in anything that's gone from Honeyford, judging from what Doran told me. It's just that . . . you won't let this go any further, old man, will you, because it could get me into a lot of trouble if it got out that I'd hinted at anything left-handed – it's just that I've heard things. Like, he's been caught out once or twice, items on the police list found in his shop, that sort of thing. That, and a rather nasty . . . but I won't go into it. All I'm saying is that Doran might have remembered something she'd heard about him and gone over there to see for herself.'

'Right. What's his name?'

'Gunterstone.' Taddeus spelt it. 'Odd name, but there it is, Phil Gunterstone. Look, don't take this too seriously. I rather wish I hadn't mentioned it. There are plenty of others, I just haven't come up with them . . .'

'Address and telephone?' Rodney did not care what Taddeus wished, a lifeline was a lifeline.

'It's 93 High Street, Tidsworth. His number's in the book. He doesn't live over the shop, so if he's gone home I can't help you about his private one.'

'Thanks, I'll ring him now.' Rodney hung up in the

middle of further protests that it was only the remotest chance.

Gunterstone's number rang insistently, monotonously, and went unanswered. Directory Inquiries could supply no other number for anyone of that name. Rodney wished passionately that he had thought of ringing Taddeus earlier.

Jane Wilford was standing beside him.

'There's a call for you on my 'phone. Owlscot police.'

Sam Eastry had been in a jumpy mood since the telephone call from Inspector Fearnlie. He was not happy with the thought of Doran on the trail of stolen antiques. She had not been arrested, she had said. That was something – but what else was happening to her? An unofficial call of reassurance from her would have been welcome. But it was not his problem, and the inspector of Owlscot had sounded competent.

Saturday afternoon brought the usual rash of weddings. Sam, off duty, assumed his other persona as Captain of St Crispin's bellringers. Up in the ringing chamber, a cheerful place on the level of the old Victorian gallery of the church, now happily demolished, he and his colleagues pulled manfully from noon until four in the afternoon. Manfully, and womanfully, for the team included two deceptively slender girls and a stout matron in her sixties. In their strong hands peal after peal rang out from the great bells, five hung before the Reformation, and one later: Evangelist, Maria, Jacobus, Paul, Jesu and Great Harry. To Sam they were his Ladies – bells, like ships, being always rated as females. They made a joyful noise of which Abbotsbourne was proud, except for a few tetchy individuals whose complaints went unheeded.

116

If they didn't like church bells, they were at liberty to go and live somewhere else.

During the services the ringers refreshed themselves with flasks of tea and packets of sandwiches. There had been a time in church history when parson and ringers had been at odds, the parson looking down on the rough characters who, he was convinced, were only in it for the beer. But Father Oliphant, now busy joining couples in wedlock, was not of that mind, and Sam, like other Abbotsbournian churchgoers, rejoiced in the ebullient man's friendliness. The Reverend Chelmarsh was much liked, and above reproach (if they'd only known! thought Sam) but Father O. seemed to throw himself into his duties as locum tenens like a two-year-old, people said. Pity he was only with them for a month . . .

The last photograph had been taken, the last bride and groom deluged with confetti. The team of ringers wiped its collective brow, coiled the sallies each in its place ready for Sunday morning, and filed down the twisting old staircase.

At the south door of the church a boy of twelve was jumping from one flat gravestone to another. Sam shouted 'Hi! stop that,' then realized that it was his son Ben.

'Dad! You're wanted. Mum sent me to tell you.'

'What's the trouble, then?'

'They phoned from Eastgate. Something about Miss Fairweather.'

'What about her? What's happened?'

'Dunno, Dad, just that you were to ring the inspector.'

Lurking in the churchyard, pretending to read epitaphs, though in fact reading was not one of his skills, Doran's gardener Ozzy hopefully watched the verger, the vicar's warden and some lady helpers go back into the church. With any luck they'd forget to lock one of the doors, and Ozzy would be able to slip in unseen when they'd all gone, and nick some flowers that he could sell at the front gate of his cottage. Easier than growing 'em. He was doing well, what with Miss Doran's garden to pick at while she was away. He hoped she would be away a good long time. . .

Inspector Burnelle of Eastgate police station had been waiting some time for Constable Eastry's return call, and said so.

'I'm sorry, sir. My son ought to have come up and told me.'

'Yes, well, he didn't. I've just had a message from Inspector Fearnlie of Owlscot, Gloucestershire. Miss Fairweather's car's been found abandoned, in woodland.'

'Oh, my God. Is she . . . ?'

'There's no sign of her, but they're looking into everything. She's been put on the Missing Persons Register. I don't suppose there's much to be got at your end, but you'd better start asking questions and let us know anything relevant – somebody may know something. Oh, and Eastry – she seems to have been with some man who's a bit of a mystery. Fearnlie says she spoke to you about him, but you didn't seem to know much. Can you find out who it was?'

Sam told him.

CHAPTER EIGHT

The Tenant of the Tomb

'Can we go over it again, sir?'

Detective-Sergeant Weller, an unsmiling North Countryman, outstared Rodney across the table. The interview room of Owlscot police station was less cosy than Inspector Fearnlie's office. It was small, bare, and smelt of stale cigarette smoke. Rodney had been shown straight down to it after a police car had collected him from the Trout. It was the classic situation: 'If you wouldn't mind stepping along to the station with us, sir . . .'

They had told him baldly of the finding of the Volvo in a tract of woodland that went largely unvisited by tourists at this time of year, lying well off the Worcester road and approached only by a rough cartway across a field not under cultivation. Stunned with shock, he had not been able to think of all the right questions to ask. No, Weller had said, there was no sign of a struggle, no traces of blood. The tank had recently been filled up with petrol. In the locked boot was luggage belonging to a woman and a man. ('My little bundle of worldly goods tied up in a spotted handkerchief.' It seemed only a few hours, and also an eternity, since he had said that to her.) Nothing seemed to have been stolen from the car.

There was also, Weller told him, watching his face, no sign of a burial in the vicinity. A pond in the woods had been dragged, but only the normal debris had been removed from it. There were no identifiable fingerprints on the steering wheel of the car, but tests were being made on the rest of the vehicle. 'Did Miss Fairweather wear gloves for driving?' Rodney could not remember, but he thought not.

'Now, sir.' The constable taking notes looked up in anticipation. Weller's voice took on a certain note when he was about to ask a crunch question. His Lancashire accent became more pronounced, and Rodney seemed to remember reading somewhere that they had rebuilt Wigan Pier and made it into a tourist attraction. He wondered if he were going mad.

'Now, sir, you'll realize that in a case like this we naturally question most attentively the person closest to the missing party. You do know that Miss Fairweather's name has been put on our Missing Persons list, I suppose, sir. We feel it very likely that you were in fact very close to Miss Fairweather. The landlady and other staff at the Leaping Trout have confirmed this. Would you have anything to say about that, sir?'

Rodney gave a sort of nod.

'But you're not married to the lady? Although you were passing yourselves off as man and wife.'

'No.'

'It seems you told Mrs Wilford at the Trout one story and Inspector Fearnlie another. Is that the case?'

'Not exactly. I . . . '

'Yes?'

'We told Inspector Fearnlie the truth.'

Weller pounced. 'The whole truth? Is your name in fact Barham? We have reason to believe it's not, from indications here and there. Would you like to add anything to that, sir? I see.' Weller turned, and raised eyebrows at the constable, who was writing a familiar formula: 'When questioned directly, refused to answer.' Weller became blunter: shock tactics.

'In cases like this there's a strong possibility of rape.

As you'll know from the newspapers it's a sadly prevalent crime. Very often rape leads to serious injuries, sometimes fatal. If that's the explanation, we've got something extremely serious on our hands. Now, according to a statement you made to Inspector Fearnlie you'd had no sort of quarrel with Miss Fairweather on the morning she disappeared. Do you still stick to that . . . sir?'

'Yes, I do, because it's true. We were . . . on particularly affectionate terms.' He was not going to tell this man about his proposal and its acceptance. 'And if, as you've discovered, we were staying at the Leaping Trout as man and wife, I'd hardly have had any need to rape her, would I – not to mince words.' Anger was mingling with distress. 'I know absolutely nothing about her disappearance, as I've told you – I only wish I did. It's a complete mystery to me, I'm absolutely stunned by it. Somebody must know something, and I've been trying to find out who.'

'I think you can leave that to us, sir. Now, we've only your word for it that you and the missing lady were on good terms . . . '

The telephone rang. Weller snapped 'Yes' into it. He had just been getting nicely into his stride. As he listened his expression changed: this, Rodney thought, was what was meant by the saying 'his face fell', for fall it literally did, out of hard lines of confidence into a despondent droop.

'Really,' he was saying. 'Yes. Yes. I've got that. All right.'

To Rodney he said, 'That call was from the chief superintendent at Eastgate. He tells me your name is Chelmarsh – the Reverend Rodney Chelmarsh, vicar of St Crispin's Church, Abbotsbourne, Kent. Is that so, sir?'

'Yes.'

'Well, that puts a different complexion on things.'

'Good.'

'I don't know why you didn't tell us that before, sir. It seems from facts ascertained by local personnel that your relationship with Miss Fairweather was of long standing, and friendly. So you've no need to answer any more questions for the moment, sir . . . '

Local personnel: that could only mean Sam Eastry. He had been putting two and two together and decided to talk. It was a certain comfort that Sam's well-known discretion was likely to keep the whole thing hushed up in Abbotsbourne, at least until some terrible tidings came which would make that impossible. And Rodney smiled grimly within himself to think that the poor old Church of England, with its bad press and growing reputation for all sorts of misdemeanours, had still some value as a character reference.

> Gates of Hell can never
> 'Gainst that Church prevail . . .

Or one passionately hoped and prayed they could not.

A heavy, clogging oppression began to clear from Doran's brain, and a noise something between ringing and buzzing gradually lessened in her ears. The murmur of innumerable. What? Bees. But not bees, which sting. She would have known if there had been bees crowding on her face. It was not bees which had made her blind.

There was some kind of pressure on her eyes, keeping them shut, and something else pressing on her mouth – or possibly only numbness, a cold insensitivity. She felt sick.

Very slowly, the noise and the sensations grew less. She became aware. Someone was speaking, out of the darkness and confusion.

' . . . shouldn't have done it, you know. I didn't expect it from anyone as pretty as you. Pretty and fragile, like a flower. I always had a weakness for big eyes and a soft mouth like a baby's. God, you're pretty, even looking like that. So sweet and helpless. You *are* helpless, aren't you, darling . . . ?'

Don't. Doran was screaming, but soundlessly; because her lips would not move. Don't dare to touch me like that. Pain and outrage gave her the strength to jerk away from the caressing, questing, probing fingers, and, later, the searching lips and the descent of a great weight on her, pinning her down. She knew what was happening but was powerless to fight it, because a tight cord held her wrists bound against her diagraphm, and the person who was trying rather successfully to rape her had pushed her arms upwards, painfully. She heard herself making muffled sounds of protest which got more and more frantic.

Suddenly the nightmare halted, as a voice said, 'So you *are*. I knew you would be. Stop it at once!'

The invader stopped. The weight lifted and she knew from the sounds that the aggressor was scrambling to his feet, and that the person who had saved her was coming nearer and speaking in a low, venomous voice.

'Trust you to have a motive. Oh, you were to make it safe for us, what else could you do? Now I see what else you're doing. Why didn't you kill her and be done with it, like you did . . . '

'Shut up.'

'I won't shut up. One law for the women and another for the men, is it? You disgust me, you know that? For all I know you had the other one.'

'It was your own bloody fault,' said the first voice, 'you *would* wear them.'

'But they were so small, too small for her to notice. She knew, without that. She'd seen them at that house. Why should she mention that thing, the horse? She knew where that came from, too. And that was you again, being stupid, letting that gipsy buy it because she fancied it, when she promised not to put it in her stock. "Gipsies and horses," you said, "fair enough."

Then this creature found it and so the old woman had to go. Now I wonder whether you pleased yourself with her, too, *cette vieille sorcière.*'

Shock had done a lot for Doran's recuperative powers. Attempted ravishment, like imminent execution, concentrated the mind wonderfully.

She knew now who the two people were, and why she was in her present ignominious position. So the French accent was put on. Cecile was French, all right, but totally bi-lingual. It could be very useful to sound sometimes French, sometimes English, as this woman could. The two of them were quarrelling noisily, a bad-tempered vicious pair, thieves falling out. Cecile was accusing Tony Taddeus of being a clumsy, impulsive fool, he throwing back jibes of carelessness at her.

'It was you thought of ether. You might have had the sense to know it wouldn't keep her under for long.'

'What else should we have used? There it was, in the workshop – did you expect me to produce a dentist's apparatus, the gas-mask or whatever they call it? If you had been enough of a man to hit her from behind you could have killed her and we should have had no more trouble. Really, Tony, you are feeble.'

'Well, I couldn't, could I? Twice is enough.' There was a shudder in his voice. 'And even if I had, we'd have had to get rid of the body.'

'That has not changed, my dear.' Cecile's tone was somewhere between a purr and a snarl. 'What do we do? The same as before?'

Doran lay very still, knowing that they were watching her. Taddeus said, 'She's fainted.'

'Don't you believe it. She's putting it on. I could bring her round very quickly – have you a match?'

'No! Leave her. She'll choke on the gag, if we're lucky.'

'I thought the ether would make her sick,' Cecile mused, 'that would have done it, all right. Come on, I'm choking myself in this place, and we shall think better in the fresh air. Leave her where she is and see what happens.'

Footsteps were going away up stone stairs, the voices remote. Something slammed heavily. A trap door falling? Then there were sounds as though a heavy weight was being dragged across a floor. Something to stop the trap door being opened from below.

She let her muscles relax as far as possible and considered her position. Cecile had been right about the lack of fresh air. There was a close, mephitic atmosphere, something between damp and decay, with a hint of dry rot in it. The ground she lay on was cold; she turned her head and felt stone under her cheek. A stone floor, with a lot of earth about. A cellar? Possibly. But in that case, what did they store in it? Surely a dealer of Tony's sort would have used every inch of storage space for his stock and restoration materials. Somebody had mentioned a workshop. But why give a perfectly good cellar over to destructive damp?

However, it mattered less to know where she was than to get herself a measure of freedom. Her hands were tied and she was gagged and blindfolded. But it came back to her that her ankles had been tied at first, and that Taddeus, in his enthusiasm for her person, had untied them. Yes, her feet were free.

Only a fool would have bound her wrists in front, rather than behind. She hoped that indicated a general ineptness on his part. Back from the past, when she had very briefly been a Ranger Guide with her school company, came the memory of reef knots and granny knots. One of them was easy to undo – but which? Doran began to twist her hands this way and that, thinking of Houdini, who had been able to slip out of the strongest fetters like an eel.

It was said he could compress his muscles and bones and organs, everything, in fact, except his skull. Doran, like a lady in a ballad, had fingers long and small. She

125

concentrated hard on compressing her right hand into the least possible compass. It was uncomfortable, then painful, and after a struggle she gave it up.

But of course – she could lift her arms, and that was obviously a priority. With her finger-ends she pulled at the eye-bandage. It had been firmly tied at the back. Twisting her head round as far as possible she worked on the knotted strip of cloth, which felt like a scarf. Some of her hair had got in with the knot, and pulling it was agonizing, but she set her teeth and persevered. Suddenly there was a slight yielding. Some determined work on the part covering her eyes got the stuff away from her cheekbones, upwards; then, with a nasty feeling that something medieval was being done to her eyeballs, she inched it upwards until it bound her forehead and at last she could see. Then it slipped off easily over the top of her head.

She was looking up at the low arched roof of what was not a cellar, but a vault. Faint grey light from high narrow gratings showed the outlines of memorial tablets on the walls. Of course: the derelict church Taddeus had talked about over dinner, the church which might become an antiques hypermarket. This was its vault – or one of them. Not a family vault, surely: too big for that. But there were recesses in the walls, too shadowed to see what was in them. Doran now knew the reason for the stench of decay, worse when she managed to slip off the gag.

By rights she should have been in a state of terror, realizing what her prison was. But what she had been through recently had frightened her far more than the proximity of old bones, which were harmless enough. She was more concerned with the living.

Rodney. What must he be thinking, feeling? Time had ceased to exist, but her watch, which she could just see, told her that it was one-fifteen. It had been a little after nine when she had sneaked off in the car, to ask Taddeus some frank questions about the Honeyford thefts. She had known Rodney would stop her, if he knew, but Taddeus had seemed so open and forth-coming at dinner – had even dropped a hint (if she cared to take it as one) that he could tell her something interesting. Perhaps he was prepared to talk. Perhaps he had an explanation about the thefts. And had made a point of giving her his card – all unknown to Rodney, who had been outside recovering from his attack of faintness.

Taddeus had not been surprised when she turned up, and Cecile had appeared, all smiles and welcome. They had expressed great disappointment when she said that she could only stay a few minutes, and Cecile had pressed her to a cup of coffee.

Over the coffee Doran came straight to the point. 'Vic Maidment. Have you any idea where he is now? I couldn't get hold of him in Eastgate. Could he possibly have sold Melody Lee that saltglaze group of the two little people, the pillion piece? And if not, who did? You see, I know he was involved in another theft . . .'

Good heavens, could anything have sounded more loaded. They must have been scared rigid. And then she had said to Cecile, 'I thought the earrings you had on last night were charming. Do tell me, are they right? I mean, I thought they looked absolutely typically Victorian, garnets set in paste. In fact, I've seen some-thing very like them in a collection of Vicky jewellery.'

Cecile had not answered for a perceptible few seconds, and had not been able to prevent her eyes from straying to her husband. Then she had said, 'So far as I know. Tony picked them up somewhere, didn't you – I think in London.'

Doran would have recognized a lie even if she had not recognized the earrings. She remembered another shared, startled glance when she had asked a question a minute before. 'Vic Maidment. Have you any idea where he is now?' An innocent question. But it had been a great red Danger sign to those two, and that was

127

why, when Cecile had gone into the kitchen, leaving her chatting with Taddeus, she had returned not with another cup of coffee but with a thick pad soaked in something sweet and overpowering which she clamped from behind over Doran's nostrils and mouth. Then there was nothing but wild visions and a buzzing in the head, and black oblivion.

Ether solvent, used for cleaning purposes, of course, in the workshop. A nice handy anaesthetic, though not one of which the medical profession would approve. But it soon evaporated, so presumably its effects on the anaesthetized person would wear off fairly quickly. Not all that much time had passed, incredibly. The crepuscular light from the gratings was not truly light, only an alleviation of the gloom; but it was just enough to see the general structure of the knot that bound her wrists.

Cecile must have plundered her scarf drawer. The eye-bandage had been patterned with horses' heads, riding-whips and horseshoes, very county, and the wrist-band was superior and silky. Wrestling with it, using her teeth, she expected to come upon the prestigious label of Jacqmar. When it finally, reluctantly yielded, she flung it away and got to her knees.

Her limbs were not especially stiff, since she had not been lying bound very long. She was cold, hollow with hunger now that the nausea had worn off, sore in places, but alive and determined to remain so, adrenalin still flowing through her bloodstream. Pretty and helpless, sweet and fragile, was she? Stone walls do not a prison make, nor iron bars a cage, even when they have a jolly good try, as this nasty place was doing.

She got up and inspected the vault. Stone steps, flanked by handrails, led up to what was presumably the body of the church. A trap-door at the top. She pushed it: it was immovable. For carrying coffins down, no doubt. Coffins. She avoided the wall alcoves, ominously full. They must all be ancient burials, but made their presence quite obvious enough. The floor was of stone flags, the vaulted ceiling cracked and breaking up at some points. Suddenly an unlikely object to find in a vault caught her eye: a light-bulb, hanging from the ceiling on a cord. And at the side of the stairs was a light switch of old-fashioned Bakelite. Incredulous, she flicked it. The vault was flooded with a radiance almost blinding after the gloom.

So far so good, better than she could have hoped. Now all she had to do was to find a weak spot in the walls or pull out a loose grating, and walk quietly and comfortably away.

But the walls were as sound as thirteenth-century builders could make them, the gratings no more than twelve centimetres deep and thirty long, to judge roughly by the eye. And in any case they were far above her head. There was nothing to stand on, unless coffins could be piled up on top of each other. The mind reeled at the thought of what might happen then. Change and decay in all around I see, observed the well-known hymn: that would be an understatement.

She paced the vault, searching for the least chance of escape. At the far end from where she had been lying a flagstone moved under her feet, rocking slightly. The one next to it was also loose. She probed the edge with a foot. The earth round them had been disturbed.

Two large flat stones, making up over two metres' length. Recently dug round – or taken up and put down again.

Doran had been cold already. Now she was ice-cold, shivering. Two stones. At his head a grass-green turf, at his heels a stone. No turf here: a headstone and a footstone, both flat. The miasma that hung on the air was very strong at this spot, something more powerful and horrible than the fetor from the old coffins.

'Vic Maidment. Have you any idea where he is now?'

She had asked the Taddeus pair that, boldly, looking them in the eye. They had known the answer, as she knew it now. Below the heavy flagstone Maidment's pale dead eyes were staring up at her, in a face rapidly changing. The long thin body must be stretched out almost beneath where she stood. Had they taken the fobs and seals he wore on a gold chain across his waistcoat, and the sixteenth-century Italian ring with the jasper intaglio? Yes, of course they had. They were thieves as well as murderers.

'Twice is enough,' Taddeus had said. Melody Lee and Maidment. But she was going to be the third.

The shivering grew uncontrollable. She was more afraid than she had ever been in her life: her regrettably short life.

CHAPTER NINE

And there's a grave within the Nave . . .

Arline Bray sat up in bed and listened. Yes, there were sounds coming from her charge's bedroom, next door to hers, through the flimsy hotel wall. She uttered a word which she was not encouraged to use at St Crispin's vicarage. It was eleven o'clock at night and she had been reading herself to sleep over a health magazine sent by her mother in Auckland, pleasantly tired after a day of swimming and surfing and an evening's strenuous table tennis.

Helena should have been asleep long ago, and here she was making some monotonous noise. Arline swung her long legs out of bed, pulled a white towelling wrap over glowing bronzed skin, and marched into the room next door.

The noise was not moaning, crying or any of the irritating sounds of which Helena was capable, but a sort of high-pitched drone.

'Well! What the hell do you think you're playing at, making that row?'

'Daddy wouldn't like you saying what the hell,' Helena replied primly.

'Never you mind what Daddy would like. Shut up, will you? Other people want to git their beauty sleep, not listen to you whining.'

'I'm not whining, I'm incanting.'

'I don't know what that is and I don't want to know.

Clam up, or I'll take the bulb out of the light and you can damn well stay in the dark.'

'Oh, please don't, Arline, you know how nervous it makes me. Arline, don't go ... What d'you suppose Doran's doing now?'

'Doran? How the heck should I know? Sleeping, I expect, like everybody in their right minds.'

Helena's eyes glinted. 'Ah, but *where*?'

'Well, at home, why not?'

'Why not, because she's with Daddy somewhere. I know you see. I can always tell when Daddy's up to something with *her*, and he had that look when he said goodbye to us. They're away together somewhere, I know they are.'

Arline approached the bed threateningly. 'You know what my ma'd do to you? Wash your mouth out.'

'All right, but he wasn't phoning from home last night, was he?'

'He was calling from a distance, on a bad line – anything wrong with that? He's driving around looking at his old cathedrals, that's all. Told me he might.'

'Cathedrals! That's a new word for it. What did he sound like when he spoke to you – happy?'

'Sort of rushed, in a hurry. I didn't take much note.'

'There, you see, he's got something on his mind. Guilt, that's it, he's doing me wrong and he knows it. How could he be happy enjoying himself with that tart, while his child suffers all alone?' Helena demanded triumphantly.

Arline, in a panther's stride, loomed over Helena, whipped off the bedclothes, turned the thin body over and administered three ringing smacks, then swiftly rolled Helena back and pulled down her nightdress. Frightened eyes stared up at her. A mouth about to shriek was covered by one large bronzed hand.

'One peep out of you,' Arline said through her teeth, 'and I'll call the night desk and tell 'em to cart you down to the basement before you wake the whole hotel, and tomorrow morning we'll be chucked out of here and you'll be taken to a hospital or maybe even the local nuthouse, and you won't like that at all, I promise you. I'm sorry I had to whack you but you just asked for it, and I'll do it again if I hear any more of that loose talk, so you watch it, will you? What you need's a shrink, not a nurse, I reckon, but your dad won't hev it, so no good me talking. He's a good guy, your dad, a damn sight too good for a kid like you.' She removed her hand, drew the bedclothes up over Helena's shivering body and tucked her in.

'You hit me,' Helena whispered. 'You hit a cripple. You're a coward and a bully and I shall tell Daddy and he'll send you away.'

'Like to bet? Come on now, off to sleep. Better hev an extra pill. Here.' Before Helena could protest the pill was in her mouth and a glass of water at her lips. She swallowed, glaring. When Arline had gone she continued to glare at the door, then swivelled her eyes round and fixed them on the dividing wall, hating through it, hating Arline.

She was not hurt, only outraged, humiliated. Now she had two people to hate. For Arline she had had a reluctant respect, the respect of a refractory animal for its master, but now that was all changed. She would go on obeying: and when the chance came she would bite.

More and more she hated Doran. It was Doran's fault that she was here with the cruel witch Arline and without Daddy, Doran's fault that she had just been smacked like a child. She had listened to some of the talk last year about evil things that had gone on in the village, and learnt that if you wished hard enough you could make accidents, trouble and suffering happen to a person far away.

Helena shut her eyes tight and wished.

*   *   *

Rodney sat by the telephone in Jane Wilford's private sitting room, his head in his hands. He was moving towards the point of exhaustion. For the last three hours, since leaving Owlscot police station, he had been trying to reach Howell Evans in Eastgate, and getting no reply.

Returning to the Trout would have been embarrassing, if he had been able to care about anything as trivial as embarrassment. Jane Wilford now knew from the police that he and Doran were not honeymooners but lovers on holiday; and it made a little, just a little, difference to her sympathies. She was not old, not even old-fashioned, only deeply conventional and romantic. In her time as an innkeeper she had been short-mannered towards unblessed couples; a deserted wife, she held all the more firmly to the ideals of wifehood.

Rodney had sensed at once the change in her feelings.

'I gather the police have been talking to you,' he said. 'If you'd rather I moved on, I will.'

She hesitated perceptibly. 'Well. It wasn't so much what they said as what they asked. I don't think you and Mrs – and your friend have been quite straight with me, have you?'

'I'm sorry, no. There were reasons, too many to explain now. But if it makes you feel better about things, we *are* going to be married – when we find her. They told you she was still missing, I imagine.'

'They didn't say a lot, you know how cagey they are. Just that the lady seemed to have disappeared and they wondered if she'd said anything to me that might give them a lead. She didn't, of course.' She was watching Rodney covertly. He was not as handsome as her James (but perhaps James had been too handsome for his own good, or hers), more what might be called nice-looking, a *good* face, very serious now and one could see the paleness under his tan, but she remembered his beautiful smile, when his lady had been with him.

No, he was certainly not a murderer, nor did he look like what her own strict mother would have called a seducer. Secretly, she knew that if she could have brought herself to divorce James, and were looking for a second, this would be the sort of man she would choose, though of course in the circumstances one couldn't allow oneself to think, even for a moment.

The cobweb bonds of sexual attraction had woven themselves round her, and she was Mr Barham's captive.

'It's absolutely awful, isn't it,' she said. 'Of course you must stay as long as you like, and if there's anything I can do, I will.'

'That's very kind of you. At least while I'm here the police know where to find me. And – if I could possibly use your private telephone. I've got to try to get hold of someone who may be a bit elusive, and you know what pay phones are like. I'll ask the operator to monitor any calls and tell me how much it all came to.'

'That's all right, my dear. I'll be serving till closing-time – we're always crowded out on Saturdays and I'm short-handed in the bar.' She patted his hand, observing the long fingers and well-kept nails. A clever hand, a hand that was nice to touch: would be nice to be touched by.

Jane, she told herself, I'm surprised at you.

A few minutes later she appeared with a tray for him, an omelette and a demi-carafe of wine. He thanked her absently as she put it down on the table beside him.

'Having no luck?' She nodded at the telephone.

'Not a lot. None, in fact. I keep persevering, however.'

'That's right. Have a glass of this, it's nothing special, but it'll do you good.' She poured some wine, which he drank mechanically. It was, in fact, something quite special, a fine Chablis of a notable year, and she had opened the bottle for his benefit.

Alone, he dialled Howell Evans's number once more. He had tried it already, countless times, without result.

He had also called Sam Eastry, found that he was out on duty, and held a long confused conversation first with Ben, then Lydia. At least he made them understand that Eastgate police headquarters must be telephoned and asked to send a constable round to Howell's cottage, to stay there until Howell appeared. Rodney was reluctant to do it, since Doran had worked so hard to keep Howell and his involvement out of the case, but desperate straits demanded desperate remedies.

Then he waited. He drank another glass of the Chablis. In his distracted state it produced in him a light-headedness in which he could think clearly for the first time about what had happened.

The dinner scene at Nina's Bistro played itself back in his mind, quite leisurely, like a slowed-down video film. Why had the Taddeii not invited them to a meal at home? He was quite sure that Cecile could cook. She was French, and therefore food-conscious, and she had made a very educated comment about the fish dish; something about its name, which set off a Shake-speare association in Rodney's mind. Sole *Clarence,* that was it, and she had remarked that it was an old and tried Prunier recipe she had at home.

So why not have cooked it for them *chez elle,* thereby saving money and entertaining in style? They owned a big Georgian house, Cecile had said. It was surely stuffed with antiques which would have interested Doran, and she would have enjoyed seeing Taddeus's workshop.

But perhaps he had not wanted her to see either his own furnishings or the workshop's contents. Was a certain damaged piece there, a horse and its two riders? Were there other pieces, things Doran would remember from the pillaged shelves of Honeyford House?

The video film moved on to freeze frame. Rodney saw himself, toying with the food, listening to Cecile chattering about something or other. He saw his hand go to the little crucifix at his neck, now hidden by a buttoned shirt and tie. And he remembered that involuntary gesture once before, when instinct had warned him of the presence of an evil personality. Tony Taddeus's big beaming face, the bland soignée woman, the light conversation – where did the evil lie?

Very light conversation indeed, when the news had just been broken to them of the murder of an acquaintance, a murder which still lay heavy on Rodney's mind. He realized now that his sudden attack of nausea and faintness had been partially psychic. Three times during his ministry he had performed the service of exorcism. Two had been at the request of neurotic house-owners whose phantoms existed in their own imaginations; the third had filled him with cold horror, the knowledge that the old ritual was fighting something real and terrible.

It had happened again. The imagined video film faded to a dot and was gone.

The Taddeii had obviously, he was now convinced, been up to their necks in theft, probably in murder. The beaming face or the bland Cranach face, or both, had looked on the dead body of the gipsy dealer: 'And someone had drawn – ah, who could it be? – a knife across her throat.' Rodney failed to remember where that came from, but it fitted his thoughts all too well. He finished the wine, shivering.

He dared not approach Taddeus directly in case he brought violence down on Doran. But the police might – if they believed him, when he had only intuition to offer as evidence of the couple's complicity. He stretched out a hand to pick up the telephone, and it rang, shocking him.

Howell's voice came across the miles. He sounded slightly drunk.

'That you, padre? I got the Old Bill here, says you want to talk to me.'

'This is Rodney Chelmarsh, yes, and I do. Where the hell have you been?'

The voice was aggrieved. 'Been down the Port Arms, 'aven't I. Anythin' wrong with that, then? Saturday night, you see, Andrew and me meet up with this couple we know . . . '

Rodney broke in. 'I don't care what you and Andrew are in the habit of doing, or when. Doran's disappeared, did you know that? Vanished without trace.'

A shocked pause. 'Disappeared? Dunno what you mean.'

'I mean that she left the hotel where we – she – where we were staying this morning and hasn't been seen since. Her car's been found abandoned. She left no message and the police are looking for her. Do you know anything about it?'

'I don't even know where you are, mate, let alone Doran. She did say she was going away for a bit—'

Rodney was simultaneously filled with white-hot fury and unnatural calm.

'She came up here, to the Stratford area, to investigate the theft of that wretched clock you pretended you'd bought—'

'I *did* buy it! I swear it on my mam's grave . . . '

'Your mam's alive and well and living in Machynlleth, so don't bother to lie to me. Whether you bought it yourself or not that clock was stolen, and I think you know where from. You'd better tell me about it, and quick, if you want Doran to be found.'

'The Bill! The Fuzz!' hissed an agitated voice into the receiver. 'I can't tell you, see – it's, well, awkward.'

'Listen to me, you little sod,' Rodney's congregation would not have recognized his voice. 'And you needn't make that scandalized noise at me. I don't use such words in the pulpit but that one's no more than you deserve. Thanks entirely to you, Doran may be in danger of her life. She's been got at by someone completely unscrupulous and vicious, who's already murdered to keep this clock business a secret. Murdered a dealer, if that's of any interest to you: she was found in her shop with her throat cut yesterday morning.'

'Oh my God!'

'Still listening? You've no need to tell that policeman anything, if he's still there. Just say you've reached me by telephone, and I told you some very bad news, and asked you to get straight into your van and drive up here. Yes, I know it's almost the middle of the night and I don't give a damn, I want you here for questioning. Either that, or you can hand the phone to your policeman and I'll tell him all I know about you *and* about the clock – which is more than you think. So which is it to be?'

'All right,' said a very subdued voice. 'Sorry to hear the bad news. I'll start right away.'

'Good. Listen, you're sober enough to drive, are you?' Howell's voice had, indeed, lost the slurring of his first words. 'How many have you had?'

'Only two. We was talking, mostly. Andrew's making tea, like he mostly does at bedtime.'

'Good. Get a pencil and paper – this is the address and how to get here.'

When he had made Howell repeat the details Rodney asked to speak to the policeman. That slightly bemused young man was easily satisfied that he was indeed speaking to the clergyman of a parish some fifteen miles away, who was investigating the disappearance of one of his parishioners, an Eastgate shopkeeper, and urgently needed the help of her business partner.

Rodney asked the operator for the cost of his calls, noted it, scribbled a line of thanks to Jane Wilford and left it beside the telephone, then made his way to bed. He felt as though he had been put through a food blender or a hand-propelled clothes wringer.

On the table beside his bed was a dainty little enamelled pill-box and a note in pretty, rounded writing.

These are absolutely harmless but awfully good. I take one myself every night and they really do work. I know you need a proper sleep. Why not try one? J.W.

Why not, indeed? Rodney smiled. Distracted as he was, he had correctly summed up Jane Wilford's situation. He thought of a long, romantic, forgotten novel, whose wandering hero unintentionally captivated a young female innkeeper. She had sent a posy – poesy – after him, with a valuable ring.

'Gyf the worlde prove harsh and colde,
Come back to the Hedde of Golde!'

He was saying the little rhyme over and over: to himself? to Doran? To her that is not here, nor doth not hear . . .

CHAPTER TEN

Lights and a Crow-bar

Solitary confinement, Doran discovered, could be monumentally boring. As one who while eating read every word on the label of a wine bottle or a marmalade jar she found the absence of anything to read almost unendurable. It took only a few minutes to exhaust the memorial tablets on the walls, which, when not too worn to be legible, were monumentally boring in a literal sense. The inscriptions on the tarnished, blackened coffin-plates in the alcoves she chose not to investigate.

What were captives supposed to do? How, for instance, did Byron's Prisoner of Chillon pass the time, apart from tramping up and down as far as his fetters allowed? She had no idea, beyond that he was rescued from madness by the song of a bird, and finally regained his freedom 'with a sigh' – as well he might. Rats: prisoners were much given to taming rats. Doran glanced round nervously. She had nothing against rats, as rats, but the thought of their company in her present circumstances was fairly unattractive.

Somebody – yes, one of the Wyatts of Allington Castle – when imprisoned and starving in the Tower of London had been visited by a cat, very fortuitously carrying a pigeon in its mouth. Wyatt got it through the bars of his dungeon window (how? it must have been an unusually amenable cat) and ate the pigeon himself. The cat returned again and again, each time with a pigeon. Freed, and back at Allington, Wyatt was thereafter very fond of cats. How he felt about pigeons in a raw state was not recorded. But there were still pigeons kept at the castle – or was it cats?

Doran realized that she was becoming light-headed from hunger. The time had crawled on to half-past four. People in the world outside were having tea; at Stratford the tourists were noshing away at their fish and chips and peas and hamburgers and cream cakes and ices.

It was bitterly cold in the vault, a damp cold that reached the bones. *Her* bones. She blanked out of her mind the thought of any others. There was an old wives' tale that if you sat on cold stone for long enough you got some distressing complaint which made future sitting very uncomfortable, and needed a painful operation. Too bad, since there was nothing else to sit on, except damp, mouldy earth. The stone steps at least gave some back support.

People imprisoned or marooned were supposed to sing, to keep their spirits up. That was feasible, and would provide a sort of exercise. The first song to occur to her was unfortunate. 'John Brown's body lies amouldering in the grave . . .' she began, and hastily stopped. 'The flowers that bloom in the spring, tra-la . . .' That was better, and led on to every Gilbert and Sullivan number she could think of. Doran having played Nanki-Poo in a school production, *The Mikado* came easiest. After that *Yeomen*, and *Pirates*, and the under-rated jewel *Ruddigore*, and *Princess Ida* with its majestic tunes . . . her voice sounded unusually good in the acoustics of the vault, as in a giant bathroom.

How very often G and S mentioned death; no plot, however frivolous, was untouched by it. She switched to the contemporary. Beatles classics were easy, and the Stones, and Bob Dylan. She meandered into country and western and folk rock. 'Farewell cold winter, and

142

farewell cold frost, Nothing have I gained, but my own true love I've lost . . . '

Her throat was hoarse and her memory growing fuzzy. She wrapped her arms round herself and walked up and down, trying to keep warmth and movement alive. Her cheeks felt colder than the rest of her; she touched them, and found them wet. It was strange to cry, without meaning to, without even knowing you were crying.

What were they going to do to her? Kill her, she supposed. At least for Melody Lee it had been quick: letting her killer in, a few words, then the knife. Or had she, being psychic, known what was coming?

Suddenly the last words Melody had spoken to Doran were illuminated, making sense at last. The red stones – she was to watch out for the red stones. Of course – the tiny garnets in Cecile Taddeus's earrings, the earrings which had twinkled a warning of villainy. Red lights – the lights have gone red. This is the red light district. No, that meant something quite different . . .

Perhaps they wouldn't kill her, though it was hard to imagine what else they could do to silence her about their two murders and thefts which obviously involved a great deal of money. The clock – that would run into tens of thousands, and Honeyford House had been a goldmine. Taddeus had masterminded the whole operation, whoever his tools had been for the actual thefts.

But of course. Cecile, so slightly-built, so Protean in appearance. Pale, undistinguished of feature, bi-lingual, something of an actress. She could have visited Honeyford in the guise of a schoolgirl, even a schoolboy, or a woman much older than her real age, stouter, of different colouring. That very short hair was ideal for being hidden by any kind of wig: a few deft touches could have transformed her. None of the stolen articles had been too heavy or bulky for a woman to remove;

the clock could easily have been fitted into a shoulder-bag of the kind tourists carried, and Doran was sure that Lady Timberlake didn't bother to have bags collected at the door and returned to their owners when they left. Taddeus might have made one or two reconnaissance visits to list the goods he wanted, though he had denied ever having seen Lady Timberlake. Cecile would have done all the thieving, and if there was a continental outlet, as Doran suspected, she was doubtless the link. The French Connection, in fact.

And Cecile would decide what to do with her, Doran. She stared round her prison for a means to leave some message that might guide searchers. A piece of stone with a sharp edge made no impression on one of the stained, time-darkened wall tablets. Her handbag had gone, leaving her without pen or paper. (Would Cecile contrive to make use of her credit cards? Very probably.)

If only she had been wearing the traditional diamond ring, which could be guaranteed to scratch a message on glass, or presumably on anything else. She looked at her hands, bare except for an attractive but valueless silver mask-ring on her right hand.

And her mother's wedding ring. It could not be used to inscribe a message, but, she thought grimly, it could be used to leave one. She slipped it off, kissed it because it had been a symbol for herself and Rodney, and read again the inscription inside: *Alice from Richard, 1956.* Rodney had seen it and he would know it again.

Steeling herself against nausea, she buried it carefully just below the top surface of disturbed earth beside one of the stones which covered Victor Maidment. Somebody would look there, some day. Perhaps they would find more bodies than one.

She went back to the steps and sat down again, leaning her head against the cold iron railing. She was very tired indeed; they had slept little the night before, their last night at the Trout, in their bridal bed.

It would be a good idea to pray, if she could only remember the right formula, woolly as her brain seemed to be. Words and phrases flitted through her mind, and some lingered, from the service Rodney loved, the service of Matins.

'Let Thy goodness and mercy lighten upon us . . .
O Lord, in Thee have I trusted: let me never be
confounded.'

Mercy touched her, sending her suddenly to sleep.

In a Georgian drawing room half a mile away Tony Taddeus was standing over his wife, his face empurpled with rage and fear.

'She's got free, don't you understand? The light's on, I could see it through the gratings. How many other people have seen it by now, tell me that?'

Cecile examined the nails she kept immaculate with colourless varnish; it didn't do to have conspicuous hands.

'What people? The place is right outside the village, not exactly Charing Cross or la Place de la Concorde.'

'How do I know? Louts glue-sniffing, having it off on gravestones, nicking lead, anything.'

Cecile giggled. 'You had me once, on a gravestone. It was funny. But on a warm afternoon, why not? However, this is not a warm afternoon. It's raining – look at your coat. I don't think many will be amusing themselves in the churchyard tonight – unless the ghosts are out. In any case, the gratings are below ground level – one has to go close up to the wall to see them.'

'You're very cool, I must say. Do you realize what this means? She's free. We'll have to overpower her before we can . . .'

145

'Kill her. Yes.' Cecile frowned. 'It's hard, to find just the right place with the knife when the person is struggling. You were lucky with Melody, she sat so nice and still.'

'There's – what we did with Maidment.'

'The cosh from behind, and then the cushion over the face. Ah, that was so easy. No. There's a trick to break the neck in one twist, but I haven't learned it, nor, alas, have you. How I wish I had a hypodermic syringe and the right stuff to put in it. You and I, we must study *le moyen juste,* if we are to go in for this sort of thing on the grand scale.'

Taddeus said, 'There's something else. Where are we going to put her – afterwards?'

'Why, there, of course, with the other one.'

'Just in case you'd forgotten, there's a community meeting on Monday night to discuss recommendations for the future of the church. Whatever's decided, they're going to send surveyors, guys with measuring gear and instruments for testing earth.'

'Not so soon, surely.'

'Soon enough. Whoever gets the site's got to know what it stands on. And they're not going to mistake Maidment for an ancient burial – nor her. Why the hell did he have to come here at all, putting the pressure on me?'

'Because his little Welsh friend let him in on it. I wish we could have got him, too – and kept the clock.' She sighed. 'But life cannot always be perfect.'

'I noticed when we were down in the vault that it's still obvious where the flagstones have been dug up, and I've got to do something to camouflage that.'

'You mean to plant little flowers around them?'

'Don't you be so bloody sarcastic!' Taddeus flared at her. 'You and I have got work to do down there, my girl. Meanwhile, I ask you, where are we going to put the woman?'

'Why, how thick you are, *chéri.* At the other place, of

course. It's perfect, so spreading, so wandering, they would not know in which bit to look – even if they knew we owned it. And the people there are used to seeing you come and go, they will not be surprised if you appear again – with stock for storage.'

Taddeus was thinking, his heavy face creased with worry. Just twice before in his career he had resorted to killing, in both cases by proxy. Doing the job himself was not to his taste, and he had not realized how difficult it is to dispose of a human corpse. His scruples were complicated by reluctance to take the life of a girl who attracted him violently, a girl with a pure Renaissance face and a body which should have been clad in flower-sprinkled gauze, like a nymph of Botticelli. He had wanted her very much.

But Cecile was ruthless, Cecile was jealous. She would do the killing. Though it might be put off a little . . .

'You realize,' he said, 'that a dead body's pretty difficult to shift? It's a dead weight – and I'm not being funny. Pretty obvious, lugging one around, if anyone caught sight of us. She's tall – it wouldn't be easy stuffing her into a sack. I'd suggest we use the ether again and keep her mobile till we get there. Besides, we don't want traces of blood around the vault.'

Cecile tilted her head, surveying him mockingly. 'One thing I will say for you, Tony – you're not a necrophile. I am glad to be married to a lecher only – I would not have fancied a monster.'

'Really? I'd have thought you'd have enjoyed it,' he said savagely. 'Come on, let's get it over tonight, before her pals come looking for her.'

Doran threw up an arm to ward off the thing looming over her, a great glossy shape, a wardrobe or press, dark red with a garish veneer. In a moment it would crush her . . .

As her dream-state faded the thing turned into Tony Taddeus's face, flushed and glistening with sweat. A voice somewhere was saying, 'Asleep! We're in luck. Be quick!'

Dawn had broken when a van pulled into the car park of the Leaping Trout. Rodney had slept in fits and snatches, never more than half-conscious. At the grating of the van's wheels on the gravel he was instantly awake, out of bed and at the window, which overlooked the park. The faint pearly light showed the van pulling up. The engine shut off and the driver stumbled out, stretched hugely, and looked about him.

Rodney was out of his room in a flash, down the main staircase and the stairs leading to the kitchens. The door from the kitchen corridor was bolted, with a heavy old iron bar across it. To Rodney ages seemed to pass as he wrenched at the bolts and lifted the bar backwards into its daytime resting place, but barely a minute had gone before he was out of the door and running towards the van.

Howell, already walking towards the inn, paused and stared. The man he had last seen lounging comfortably in Doran's garden wore only short pyjama pants and spectacles, but Howell had a good visual memory.

'The Reverend, isn't it?' His voice was harsh with tiredness and smoking.

'Yes. You made it, then – well done.'

'I set off just after you phoned. That young cop went on a bit about how I oughtn't to drink-drive, but Andrew swore I'd had next to nothing, nor I had, really. Very persuasive, Andrew can be. *Duw*, I'm knackered.' He stretched again. 'Dunno how many miles, but it bloody seemed like Round the bloody World in Eighty Days. Lucky for me there wasn't much on the motorways – Sunday, you see. Look, you got next to nothing on – no slippers even.' At any other time his glance would have been admiring.

'Nor I have. Doesn't matter. Come on up to my room. There's nobody else about yet.' As they walked, Rodney was conscious of the gravel cutting into the soles of his feet; he had not been aware of it before, so the fire-walkers' principle of absorption in higher things must be valid. He saw in the growing light that the Welshman's face was haggard and unshaven and his expression sombre.

Rodney's small room was equipped with facilities for making tea and coffee. Howell drank thirstily, then put down his half-emptied cup.

'What about Doran?'

'No more news, nothing. But then you don't know what's happened.' Succinctly he outlined the events of the past seven days. He made no comment on his presence in the district, or on how he and Doran came to be staying at the Trout together. Nor did Howell.

Howell lit a rank cigarette, puffed at it, threw it away and lit another one. His hands shook and his face was tense under the grime of his journey. When Rodney had brought the story up to date Howell stubbed out his third fag in the washbasin and swore, softly, comprehensively, in some words Rodney knew and others he did not, to his surprise. Howell cursed in both English and Welsh, dealt his own right cheek a stinging blow with his fist, and subsided.

'What was that for?' asked Rodney.

'For me. For being a stupid soddin' fool. If I'd had the guts to say no, none of this'd ever have happened.'

'You'd better tell me about it.'

Howell told him. The tale he had spun when showing them the clock had been a pack of lies, as Doran had guessed. When he and Andrew had moved into the Warwickshire area they had known Victor Maidment would be there as well, doing some prearranged deal. They met at a pub which Maidment thought to be

149

something of a safe house. He told them the broad outline of the deal: he had agreed to convey the loot from a country house robbery to Dover and get it across the Channel to contacts who would be waiting at Calais.

'Contacts of Cecile Taddeus's.'

'Right. He wasn't goin' to show me nothin' – it was all in his van packed up. But then he mentioned the East clock, and that got me where I live – you know me and clocks, at least Doran does. I made him show me it – and I got him to part. God knows how. I gave him all the cash we had with us, all but enough for petrol to get us home, and promised him more when we met up again. I daren't have told Doran how much . . . '

'What you did tell her was that you had a buyer lined up.'

'I had. I have. I'd love to keep it, I'm crazy about it, but I don't want anythin' as hot as that on the premises. Not after Vic didn't come back.'

'Didn't come back where?'

'To Eastgate. Last we saw of him, after he'd sold me the clock, he said he was off to see this Taddeus and pick up another biggish piece Taddeus got off another guy in the Ring at an auction – coffer, guy thought it was pussy-cat but Taddeus knew it was early sixteenth.' Seeing Rodney's baffled expression, Howell translated this as meaning that the other dealer had mistaken the piece for the sort of Victorian furniture known as pussy-cat oak, from the machine-cut lions' heads usually ornamenting it, but that Taddeus had recognized it as early Tudor.

'He was coming home after that. But he never did. Nobody's heard a thing. His flat's shut up, no orders to the milkman nor no one. Not even Graham's heard – that's his fem.' Rodney knew better than to ask for another translation. 'Taddeus has got a name.'

'For what?'

'Bent gear. And . . . other things.'

150

'And has his wife got one?'

Howell's face went still. 'Nobody likes to say much about *her*. She keeps very quiet, but from something Vic let drop . . . And they've got Doran. Oh God, oh God, what am I going to do?' The red-rimmed eyes were swimming in tears. 'I love that girl, you know, mate, I mean Rev, not the way you do but I love her even though I don't show it a lot.'

'So I gathered. I mean that you don't show it much, but I believe she's got you in the heart-of-gold category. Well, never mind your feelings or mine – and by the way, you needn't bother calling me Rev or Reverend or anything – my name's Rodney. What matters is finding out where Doran is and getting her back. Urgently, like now.' He looked at his watch. 'Half-past four. We'd better start. Your van's OK, is it – got enough petrol?'

'Filled up at an all-night station. How far are we going?'

'About fourteen miles, maybe a bit more. Place called Lippett Green. Give me two minutes to get dressed. Bathroom's across the corridor, and be quiet about it.'

In view of Howell's exhaustion, Rodney decided to drive. As they pulled out into the lanes still empty of traffic in the dawn-mist he told Howell as much as he could recall about the dinner conversation at Nina's Bistro. 'He told me they'd got a big Georgian house with stockroom and workshop attached. That suggests out-buildings, so we'll have a shufti round those first, as we obviously can't go beating at the door at this hour.'

'Why not? No time for standin' on ceremony, is it?'

'Absolutely right, Howell. I just have this feeling that we ought to look for ourselves first.'

Somewhere Doran was a captive, but it didn't do to brood on that. Rodney used his own habit of discipline to think of nothing but negotiating the bends of narrow lanes, anticipating the approach of vehicles more familiar with the district, and wondering, practically, what time they could expect to find some breakfast. Howell was silent, his deep depression filling the van in rivalry with its pungent atmosphere. And serve him right, God forgive him. Rodney wound down the window and breathed Cotswold air.

A signpost pointed to Lippett Green, half a mile. Rodney slowed down and jogged Howell's side. 'Watch out for a house called Baker's Ley.'

'Wha'?'

Rodney spelt it. 'I found it in the phone book. And their number, if we need it.' He hoped Howell was going to be some use. His eyes were still watery and he looked like a man on the way to execution.

A house or two appeared, two or three shops, a post office. A cluster of picture-postcard cottages, a filling station, an amorphous hut-like building with miscellaneous notices for local functions posted outside it. Then they were facing the open road again, Lippett Green behind them.

'Blast,' said Rodney. Howell clutched his elbow, suddenly and dangerously.

'There it is! On that gate, set back.'

And there it was, Baker's Ley, a tall doll's house of a building behind high walls and big double gates. Rodney stopped the van, got out and tried them. They were locked as firmly as gates could be. A bell set in one gatepost said, 'Visitors' with a notice of a burglar alarm system above it. He said, 'Blast!' again. The only way of surmounting those walls would be by the same means as those a prisoner with good friends outside would use to escape from Parkhurst.

The house's curtains were drawn. It had the air of a place which would awake only in its own time. Lippett Green itself was beginning to come to life; a milk-float rattled past, and somewhere a dog was barking monotonously. The hour was advancing, and they must act soon.

'Come on – we're too conspicuous.' Rodney returned to the van and drove it several hundred yards past the gates, parking it under cover of a high hedge. 'Now,' he said, 'we'll go and investigate the back of the place. I've never met a wall that didn't have more than one break in it.'

All round the boundaries of Baker's Ley was open land, the nearest cottage too distant to qualify as a neighbour. At the back the prospect was open as far as a range of hills, already touched by sunshine: and at the back was also a gap in the walls, a high farm gate, and a view of the rear of the house.

It had been added to, clearly in recent years, by buildings on a lower level than the original one, functional buildings of concrete, joining on to older ones of stone which might have been dairies or laundries. A double garage had a large shabby estate car and a plain tradesman's van standing outside it. A number of tea-chests were stacked against one wall.

'Well,' said Rodney, 'we'd better climb over and see what the means-of-entry situation's like.' His long legs were over the gate before Howell's short ones had managed more than the second bar. 'Don't you bother,' Rodney told him. 'One can get round quicker than two.'

He came back dejected. 'They don't mean anyone to get in there without the password. I'd say the main door to the workshop's photo-electric, and the others are double-locked. Alarm notices everywhere.'

'Colditz, like.'

'Colditz.' Rodney said under his breath, ' "Show Thy pity upon all prisoners and captives." '

'So what do we do?'

'There's a back door. We ring the bell and wait. Come on.'

'What if they jump us when they open the door?'

'My dear Howell, why should they? They only know

153

me as a friend of Doran's, and Taddeus will hardly be expecting you – it would be a bit impetuous to knock us out first and ask questions after. We'll act normally, and so, I imagine, will they – whoever answers the door.'

Howell grunted. 'We got nothing to hit back with if they did, though. Suppose it was one of them big bruisers, like in the films. Your hands wouldn't be much good against a professional chucker-out, nor would mine.' He displayed surprisingly small and delicate fingers. 'We ought to have a weapon of some sort.'

'Curiously enough—' Rodney pulled something from his jacket pocket. It was a small bust, about the size of a man's fist, representing a Red Indian brave with a feathered headdress and an implacable expression. Howell took it to examine, almost dropping it.

'Gor, what a weight! What's it made of?'

'Carborundum. Silicon carbide. About the hardest known substance, apart from iron. Note the sharp corners, very good for denting heads. Handy little thing, isn't it. A paperweight. I picked it up off a desk in the pub parlour. In case it came in useful.'

Howell was silent; his opinion of clergymen was altering rapidly. Rodney, climbing back over the gate, surveyed the valley behind him. Three fields away a square church tower rose. Rodney realized with a shock that it was Sunday morning. In two hours or so people would be going to early service, Holy Communion at eight o'clock. At home, Father Oliphant would be still asleep in his, Rodney's, bedroom, soon to wake and prepare for the first rite of the day; doubtless without breakfast, good man. Perhaps even in this quiet place a single bell would ring to summon Cotswold folk.

With a sharp jolt memory took him back to the dinner conversation with the Taddeii. The church

154

affair, Taddeus had said; a small disused church, which might be demolished and used for building or turned into an antiques supermarket. St Faith's, that was it. He had asked whether it had been deconsecrated, and Taddeus had not known.

In the mild morning air, Rodney was suddenly cold from head to foot. He climbed down to rejoin Howell.

'Come on,' he said. 'Hurry.'

'Where? Where we goin'? I thought we was . . .'

Rodney, striding ahead towards the car, made no answer.

St. Faith's looked as disused as a church could be. Its small graveyard was overgrown with brambles and weeds, many panes of glass were missing from its windows, where vandals had thrown stones. The stout studded door of the south transept had once been locked, but someone had smashed it in, leaving only the great ring-handle swinging forlornly.

Howell, with a confused notion in his head that his companion was obeying some religious urge, followed him inside. He was not a frequenter of churches, but it was obvious even to him that this one was in a poor state. Everything of value had been removed. The bare altar stood without ornaments.

'Even the lectern's gone,' Rodney said. 'Because it was brass, I suppose.' He went to the west end of the nave and looked up into the bell tower. No chime would ring from it again, for the bells were gone. The undistinguished pews were late Victorian, the pulpit matched them. On the walls stone tablets bore a few time-eroded skulls and cupids, and two funerary hatchments had been left in the rood-loft, possibly because they were too high up for convenient removal. Poor St Faith had little credibility left.

Rodney was examining the flooring, an ugly tessellated surface which had replaced any floor slabs there might have been. Howell tagged unhappily along behind him.

'What you lookin' for, then?'

Rodney did not answer. He had progressed into the north-east corner of the chancel. In a small side-chapel two pews had been displaced, dragged aslant so that two ends were together. Beneath, the tessellation showed a four-sided break some five feet square, with two iron rings on the nearest edge.

'Trap door,' said Rodney. 'Somebody didn't want it noticed. There has to be a vault under here. Nothing in the churchyard that could be one, and no other use for these rings. Come on, get these pews off it.' They were heavy and cumbrous. Rodney grasped one of the iron rings, Howell another. 'Heave!' Rodney ordered.

The slab began to rise, yawned wider and wider, until Rodney was able to rest it, upright, against the wall. Howell, awed, looked into the dimness below them, where broad stone steps with a handrail each side led downwards. Rodney was already starting down them. 'Got a match?' he called up. Howell handed him a box.

By the thin light of one Rodney reached ground level, struck another, and saw the electric switch. He flicked it, bringing the underground chamber to life and looked round, seeing with enormous relief not what he had feared to see but a blank empty crypt. 'Come on, it's all right,' he called.

Howell was not feeling at his best. He was tired out, hungry, gasping for a coffee or a Scotch, nauseated by the fetid breath of the vault. He was also superstitious with the superstition of a Celt, fearful of the presence of dead bodies. Too young to have been in the war, even to remember the falling of bombs, he had never seen a corpse in his life, and here he was surrounded by them: not that any were visible, but there were nasty shapes in the wall alcoves about which he guessed accurately.

He should have sworn violently, stamped out of the place and driven off to the nearest town, leaving the mad parson to his own devices. But there was no mad parson, only a desperate man searching for Doran; and Howell knew that he must stay and help.

'OK, Rod,' he said, descending.

Rodney was standing staring at the ground beneath his feet, his face like a mask of stone.

CHAPTER ELEVEN

Blood calls for blood – 'tis Heaven's decree!

'Christ!' he said. It was the first time he had used that name outside its professional connotation.

Howell's eyes followed his to the two slabs and the line of newly-turned earth round them.

'Oh my God,' he said, over and over again. Then, 'They haven't, have they? The bastards, the bloody bastards.'

'Go and find a phone box.' Rodney's voice did not sound like his own. 'Call the police. Get them here.' He dropped to his knees and began to prise at the edges of the stones. Howell went, swiftly, not looking back. If it were true, there was little point in hurrying, but it seemed to be all he could do, except stay in that horrible cellar.

The call-box outside Lippett Green's post office had been vandalized, but unsuccessfully. Surrounded by graffiti, fag-ends and worse, Howell dialled. He had to repeat his information several times before it was understood, for emotion had brought on his accent to the point of foreignness. At last the message got through. He went back to the van and puffed at three cigarettes before returning to St Faith's.

Rodney was still kneeling, scraping at the earth with a corner of the paperweight. He did not look up as Howell appeared.

'They're on their way,' Howell told him. They were more than that, they had arrived and were following

159

each other down the steps, four men whose large presences seemed to crowd out the vault. They carried spades and something hammer-shaped which Rodney supposed was a mattock. Give me that mattock and the wrenching-iron ... why I descend into this bed of death Is partly to behold my lady's face ...

'If you wouldn't mind, sir.' A sergeant was gently pushing him aside, out of the way of those who were raising one of the stones, and raising it with surprising ease and speed. It was up, freed, placed elsewhere. The four policemen and Howell were looking down at a thin layer of earth scattered loosely over something that had been put into a very shallow grave. One of them brushed it aside, revealing features which interment had not improved, but Howell recognized them. In a flash he was at Rodney's side, where he leaned against the wall, his eyes shut.

The torrent of Welsh and English he poured out was incoherent, but the message got through to Rodney. Howell's arm was round his shoulders, he was being pulled to the graveside, urged to inspect its contents.

'Who the hell's that?' he managed to say, before the sergeant was at his side with a pocket flask of brandy. Rodney was shocked to hear himself laughing.

'Hold up, sir. Just sit down there for a few minutes. You too, sir, please.'

'It's Vic Maidment!' Howell was saying. 'I told you he never come back. That Taddeus done him in, see, poor old sod, but at least it's not Doran – don't blame you for thinkin' it was, I did myself, come out in a proper sweat.' He wiped his brow. 'Can I have a swig of that? Ta. Now you get yourself together, *bach,* we got to keep our heads and find Doran.' He finished the contents of the flask, gulping.

Rodney smiled, something which a few moments ago he had not expected to do again. 'Yes, we have. You're a tower of strength, Howell. Thanks.' They watched as the policemen got the body out of its grave and busied themselves with examination. After a few minutes the large, placid-faced sergeant joined them, leaning on the stair rail.

'Well, that's it, gentlemen. No clues to identity, keys, cards, nothing.'

'He had a nice lot of old seals and fobs,' Howell said. 'Used to wear 'em on a watch-chain – pretty, they were – and he always wore a big heavy ring with a cardinal's head cut into a jasper stone. What's become of them?'

'What, indeed, sir. But as you recognize the deceased we'd better go along to the station and get it all down on paper. Oh, and we turned this up among the earth.' With one thick forefinger he dusted soil away from the gold ring. 'Would it have any connection, d'you think?'

He was speaking to Howell, but it was Rodney who snatched the ring and read the inscription: *Alice from Richard, 1956.*

'No,' he said, 'but I know whose it was – is. Somebody else has been kept down here . . . ' he looked wildly round the floor space.

'Nobody else here now, sir, not underground, nor in the churchyard – one of the lads has had a look round. No sign of another recent burial and nowhere in the church a body could be hidden. Let's get going, shall we?'

Rodney gazed round the interview room at Owlscot police station, thinking he had never seen a friendlier, more homely place. That had not been his impression on his first visit, but now the world was wearing a brighter aspect than it had done for some time. They had been given a large if greasy breakfast of eggs, bacon, tomatoes and toast, washed down by quantities of tea out of a machine. Detective-Sergeant Weller, summoned from an intended morning of gardening, had greeted Rodney with a weary smile.

'Mr Barham – again? But it's the Reverend Chelmarsh, of course. We've got a fair bit to sort out, haven't we?'

'She *must* be alive,' Rodney insisted. 'She left that ring as a message, surely.'

'It could have come off accidentally,' said Weller.

'Impossible. It was nearly too small for her – she'd have had to wrench it off. She buried it just under the earth, so that when Maidment was found it would be found, too.'

'That could have been a long time . . . And if she did, it still doesn't tell us where she is now. Definitely not at Taddeus's home – we've searched it from attic to cellar and found no trace of anyone, alive or dead.' Weller did not say what else they had found, in the way of antiques on the Stolen List, which had caused him to take Taddeus's activities very seriously, and raised grave doubts in his mind that any person who had got in the man's way would be left alive to tell tales. He kept this, too, to himself. His two witnesses had taken enough for the time being. Howell Evans had declared that he must crash out or become another corpse on their hands, and he was doing just that in the back of his van, becalmed in the Sabbath peace behind the station.

Rodney had been thinking intensively. 'They had another place,' he said. 'It was mentioned at dinner that night. I didn't take a lot of notice because I wasn't feeling well, but I think Taddeus said it was a flat. Can you find out where it is?'

Weller shook his head. 'Difficult, on a Sunday. From what my lads have picked up they weren't exactly matey with anyone in the village – kept themselves to themselves. They'd been in the area around four years, but their friends all seemed to be in the antiques world – nobody local. With a search warrant we could go through documents in the house, of course, and something might come to light, but it'll all take time.' He did

162

not add that in his opinion they had very little time, perhaps none.

Rodney beat his brow. 'If only I'd listened! The woman said something about a different style – of what, house, furniture? Can't remember. Baker's Ley is Georgian so it could have been anything else . . . '

Weller was uninterested in style. 'These dealer friends, I suppose you don't know any names, or where we could locate them?'

'Not a clue. Four years. Did you say the Taddeii – the Taddeus couple had been here four years? That means the house and the flat must have been taken on quite recently. What about estate agents? They'd know.'

Weller quenched the light of enthusiasm that shone in his witnesses's eyes. 'Again, not on a Sunday, sir. They don't tend to live over the shop.'

'Try, just try! Isn't there one particular firm that handles properties in the district?'

'Well, there's Chepstow's, but . . . '

Rodney sensed the pessimism behind Weller's tone, the ready abandonment of hope by a man who as a young constable had searched for lost children and found them on patches of waste ground or in the basements of derelict buildings, within half a mile of home. He fought it with his own belief.

'Find someone. Even on Sunday, in August, someone will know. Please!' In a working lifetime of prayer he had never made one so passionate. Weller shrugged. Simple faith in action, he supposed. He picked up the local telephone directory.

Far south in Abbotsbourne, Father Oliphant was putting on his surplice in the vestry of St Crispin's. He paused, admiring the play of a sunbeam through crimson stained glass, and hoped that the vicar whose place he was taking was enjoying a pleasant and restful holiday.

*　　*　　*

163

For Doran the nightmare was beginning again. She was struggling out of a stupor, the fumes of ether in her head and lungs, fighting nausea and giddiness, the same two voices in her ears that had been raised in quarrel before. But this was not the vault, nor was she bound, blindfolded or gagged. She was lying on the carpeted floor of a beamed and panelled room, and the ether must have been carelessly administered this time, since she could remember a car journey, and being carried upstairs. The room was lit by a standard lamp, soft radiance after the glare of the vault.

The Taddeii were arguing. Cecile was standing like a fishwife, arms akimbo, facing up to the big man. From his appearance Doran would not have laid odds on him in any fight that might be going to happen. He looked as if he were about to go off in an apoplexy, as the obituary makers used to put it; his eyes were red-shot and his jowls sagged and quivered.

'Then get on with it!' Cecile shouted. 'We lost enough time with that flat tyre, the whole bloody thing should be over by now.'

'Shut up, you'll waken everyone in the house. Just give me time and I'll do it. I can't get my breath properly . . . all those stairs . . . '

'Your breath, you great ox – what has that to do with it? Just one blow –'

Doran heard this fierce exchange with the non-comprehension of someone aware of a television drama going on, but not looking at the screen. She felt light-headed, curiously detached, as though none of it were to do with her. Then, raising herself on her elbow to watch, she saw Cecile close with Taddeus and wrench something from him, something that glittered. He shrieked.

'You've cut me, you bitch!' Blood was dripping from his wrist.

'I'll cut her, too!' his wife shrieked back. 'I'll mark her so they won't know her pretty face when they find her,

164

because you fancy her, don't you, you lecher? *Taureau, libertin, sale chien! Tu veux foutre la salope, n'est ce pas?* That's why you won't finish her yourself. I shall do it for fun, *pour m'amuser.*'

'No, don't!' Taddeus was pleading, sucking his bleeding wrist, clutching her arm with his other hand. 'Cecile, don't!'

'You beg for her, you didn't beg for the gipsy, eh? I'll show you how they mark cows with big eyes and little *tetons*, slash, slash, slash . . . '

Oh, come, thought Doran, not as little as all that, and look who's talking. She watched with her new strange detachment. Suddenly Taddeus turned his head and met her look with one of desperation. Not knowing why, she smiled at him. He was, after all, defending her, in his way.

His face changed and he turned away, his back to her, blocking her view. There was a choking, bubbling cry as Cecile fell. The awful sounds stopped after a moment and her head rolled sideways, eyes staring and blood pouring from her open mouth.

Taddeus stood looking down at her, the storm that had shaken him suddenly past. Then he came over to Doran. But he had left the knife where it had fallen, beside Cecile.

'I can't do it, you know,' he said gently. 'She was quite right. Should never have started all this. The others were something else, but I can't bear to kill anything beautiful. Beautiful things, they've been the ruin of me. I'm going to make a run for it now with what I can. I wish I could take you with me.' He knelt beside her, the bloodshot eyes liquid with tears. 'I'm sorry . . . about everything.'

'Don't mention it,' said Doran. He bent and kissed her, with expertise and violence.

Her hand at her bruised lips, she watched as he effortlessly scooped up Cecile's body and threw it over his shoulder. She had been small in life; in death she seemed to have shrunk even further. Without glancing at Doran again, he went out of the room, shutting the door behind him.

Long ago Doran had rescued a mouse from a cat. The mouse had been quite unharmed, merely damp from the cat's mouth. It had sat up on its haunches and felt itself all over to make sure that it was intact, then dashed away before, as it probably anticipated, its rescuer could appropriate it for herself and eat it.

She knew how the mouse had felt; only she had not the strength to get up and run. She was shaking uncontrollably, just able to prop herself up on one elbow, trying not to look at the blood on the dark gold carpet. In other circumstances the room would have been pleasing with its panelling, pale ancient oak, and it's well-chosen furniture. Jacobean, original, not pussy-cat? The carved fireplace surround had androgynous supporters, creatures with well-developed breasts and luxuriant beards, mermaid-like tails that merged into cornucopia over-flowing with fruit and grain.

It was all oddly familiar. She had been talking to someone about this room. Or a room like it, in her imagination. A room in a house they had seen, she and Rodney.

The window was diamond-paned. All the windows visible from the road were like that. Interesting that some of the glass was old. She was incapable of reaching it, but she knew that it would look on to a moat, that there would be an older wing behind the Jacobean front of the house, and a farm cottage with hens strutting in the yard. She was in the house she and Rodney had called the Moated Grange.

If only she could crawl to the door – Taddeus hadn't locked it. But even her brain was working inefficiently. Though well enough to remember Jane Eyre hearing, far off, Rochester's voice calling her name: and answering him. That was fiction, of course. But if one will it very hard, with all one's strength, perhaps such a miracle might be able to happen.

Rodney, oh, love, please find me.

She collapsed again, and lay where she had fallen.

'. . . yes, I see. Extremely helpful. Thank you very much, sir – sorry to disturb you on a Sunday.' Weller turned from the telephone with a cheerful face. 'There's a turn up for the book, Mr Chelmarsh. I got hold of Mr Chepstow junior at home and he was able to give me the address of Taddeus's flat. It's . . . '

'I know,' said Rodney. He wore a strange expression – awestruck, mystic? Weller did not recognize it.

'You *know*, sir?'

'Not the address. But what the house is like, where it is. Not very far from here.'

Weller said nothing as he left to inform the CID men who had been called in on the hunt. He was beginning to think of himself as being involved not merely in simple robbery and murder, but in the Case of the Curious Clergyman.

Stanisley House, the Moated Grange's real name, was surrounded by police, uniformed and plain-clothes. It was also surrounded by the dwellers from the maison-ette above the Taddeus's flat, and the farm-workers from the cottage, all adding their contributions to the mêlée. Weller and his attendant constable were sorting out their statements, which seemed to add up to a heavy degree of Sunday morning sleep. The maisonette owners slept on the top floor, and had heard nothing until the arrival of the police cars, the cottager's wife had got up to feed the chickens and gone back to bed after noticing vaguely that the Taddeus estate car was standing in the stableyard. Two men were breaking down the heavy door that led from it into the house.

A shout came from one of the CID men. 'Woman's body in the moat.' His colleagues rushed to join him, and Howell said to Rodney. 'Steady on, don't panic.' Then they were looking into the still waters edging the ragstone walls of a round tower, and a small form in what had been elegant trousers and a St Laurent top, floating on its face, held by weeds that moved languidly round it.

'I told you, see,' said Howell.

'That's Mrs Taddeus!' shrieked the cottager's wife. 'Oh look, there's blood . . . all over her. Oh, poor thing. Eric, do come and see, it's dreadful!'

Rodney ran upstairs behind the two who had broken down the main back door. At the top of it was another door, unlocked, and beyond that a kitchen, well appointed with the most modern of equipment – a Frenchwoman's kitchen. Superlative Seurat reproductions and a Jean Dupas Underground poster ennobled white walls. Beyond the kitchen was a passage leading to a door in an older wall. Rodney raced ahead to it, the two young officers hard on his heels.

He was across the room before them, gathering Doran into his arms, saying her name over and over, and other things which were incoherent. Detective-Sergeant Bowra jerked his head at his colleague.

'Out. Give 'em a minute.'

At Owlscot police station – the Old Nick, as Doran now affectionately thought of it – they were restored to something like their normal selves after an interlude over the edge of uncontrollable emotion, though Rodney still found it difficult to relinquish Doran's hand. Her mother's wedding ring had joined the collection of police exhibits.

She had been fed, reunited with her car, driven to Weller's tidy little house and looked after by his comfortable wife. A bath and a change into clean clothes from her suitcase had done wonders for her. A recap of the day's events had taken place in the presence of the head of the local CID.

Detective-Inspector Malcolm Treece disapproved of the cosy atmosphere. Of a cynical nature, he had no confidence in clergymen simply because they were clergymen, or in antique dealers of any kind. There was, in his view, which he had already shared with Weller in private, something distinctly fishy about the whole set-up. He did not believe for one second that Rodney had suddenly been inspired by extra-sensory perception or anything else to realize that his girlfriend was being held at Stanisley House; not that it mattered, since the address had already been traced, but the police should not be told silly pointless lies for the sake of effect, which must have been the reason for this one. Treece had not a single superstitious cell in his entire nervous system, and had no intention of cultivating any.

The girl. With that dreamy, fairy-princess face and those big eyes, she could get away with almost anything. She'd certainly been put through a hell of a lot, but how much had she asked for, Treece wondered. She had brains enough to spin webs of deceit round facts, if it suited her; and his instinct told him that she was concealing something.

And Evans. Another dealer, and a bent one – Treece had the nose of a tracker dog sniffing out cocaine, when it came to bent dealers. Howell had recognized the murdered Maidment, and Maidment had known Taddeus, and Taddeus's house had been a treasure cave of articles which were on the police lists of stolen property – and that was only local. No doubt plenty would prove to have come from more widespread robberies. The saltglaze pillion piece had been there, the piece for which Melody Lee had been murdered because she'd been unwise enough to display it in her shop, and a number of recognizable antiques from

169

Honeyford House. (They had telephoned Lady Timberlake, asking her to come and identify her property, but she had only gibbered and hung up on them.)

In Treece's book, when seemingly innocent parties turned up repeatedly in connection with known criminals, the law was entitled to take an interest. He did not think Doran Fairweather had visited Honeyford House by coincidence. Birds of a feather flock together, you can spot a wrong 'un by the company he keeps, and these three were all wrong 'uns in their way. There was nothing on which he could hold them, unfortunately; but when they got back to their home base they would be kept under close observation. Especially Evans.

But at least he would have Taddeus soon. 'We've got an alert on the Channel ports,' he informed Weller, 'and the airports – not that he'd be likely to take his loot out that way. His estate car's gone and you can bet it's full, wherever it is. He must have scooped up the best stuff before he left in a hurry. Bloody idiot, losing his nerve and knifing the woman – he could have managed things a lot better.'

'Like, knifing me and taking his time over escaping?' Doran opened her eyes wide at him. He stared back coldly.

'If you care to put it like that.'

'He didn't believe a word we said,' she told Rodney when, later, they shared a tray of tea in the bedroom of their hotel, far south of Owlscot and on the route back to the motorway. It was an Edwardian house sensibly converted to hotel use, furnished with taste and cheerful chintzes. Their bedroom dazzled with white paint and glowed with curtains and duvet-cover of a large poppy print.

'I know that. He certainly didn't believe Weller about my knowing you were at the Moated Grange. I almost don't believe it myself.'

170

Doran was not sure whether she did or not. She had been concentrating on making Rodney find her, remembering the message that had flashed between Jane and Rochester, before the invention of radio or the telephone. Perhaps she and Rodney had both been over-tense and imagined things. It was more important to be practical.

'Taddeus won't make straight for a Channel port – not directly, if he's any sense, and he's not an utter fool.'

'Only mad nor'-nor'-west. So what will he do?'

Doran ate half an egg sandwich, meditating. 'I'll tell you what *I* think. He'll hide up until the trail's cooler. And where, you ask? Not difficult. There was nothing on Vic Maidment's person when they found him – right? So Taddeus has Vic's documents of identity – his address, keys, everything. If I were Taddeus I'd go to earth in Vic's flat.'

'Which the cops will search, surely.'

'Which they'll already have searched, if I know them. They got his address out of Howell this morning. The Eastgate boys will have been over it already with a photographer and fingerprint powder and the lot. As there's no mystery about his killer they probably won't have sealed it off or left anyone on watch – why should they? So the coast will be clear by the time Taddeus gets there – and he's had all day to do it in.'

'Driving a van they're looking for?'

'One imagines he's heard of fake number-plates, with his experience – probably got wardrobes of them in those outbuildings you saw. I wouldn't put it past him to have swapped vehicles near the start of the journey. What happened to Vic's car, for instance? He was killed at Baker's Ley, so it must have been parked nearby. Mark my words, they'll come across Taddeus's van parked somewhere and it won't occur to them to look out for Vic's.'

'Ingenious. What are we supposed to do about it?'

'Find him before they do.'

'For heaven's sake, why?'

'It would be such a triumph – a piece of one-upmanship on the unbeliever Treece.'

Rodney set down his cup with a clatter. 'I never heard such an utterly wild idea in my life. After all the danger you've been in, all I've been through, you calmly contemplate walking into that murderer's hands again, and getting yourself killed properly this time. Well, I won't have it, do you hear? I won't lend myself to it, and you're not going anywhere without me, so get that straight, will you? If Taddeus is at Maidment's flat he can stay there, and I for one shall be pleased to point the police at him. You weren't thinking of warning him, by any chance?'

Doran responded to heavy sarcasm with raised eyebrows. 'No, no. Though I do owe him, I suppose, for not killing me. I think what he had in mind was more of a *coup de foutre* ... – *so to speak*. Oh darling, darling, don't look like that, I didn't mean to upset you – I just can't help being flippant. Reaction, or something. Come here. We won't say another word about it. I'm really very tired and I think I should like to lie down. What about you?'

But in the back of her mind a plan remained. In all the investigations not a word had been spoken about Rose Hathaway's clock. If she were clever, the police need never know about Howell's involvement with it.

> Rose Hathaway, she hath a way
> To ...

To what? Or was it Anne, not Rose? Doran had not intended to waste the evening sleeping, but exhaustion suddenly caught up with her. Rodney gently covered her up and let her sleep into the night, himself staying on guard for an hour in case Howell should take it into his head to wander out of his single room and visit them for conversation and bottle-sharing.

But the night was still, only the sounds of distant traffic drifting through the open window. In the single room, surrounded by bright blue print cornflowers, Howell was dreaming of the clock.

CHAPTER TWELVE

The Prime of The Swag

Doran pulled the car in on the forecourt of the Downs Service Station.

'Well, here we are,' she said flatly. 'This is where we part company and you drive chastely back to the vicarage and tell Father Oliphant how much you enjoyed the Harrowing of Hell.'

'I will. I did, at the time – the one on the north transept wall, that is. It was the real thing I didn't much care for. Oh dear.'

'Oh dear.' They looked long at each other. Doran said, 'Don't kiss me. There's bound to be an attendant with eyes all round his head. We've got away with it nicely so far – don't let's push our luck.'

She watched him disappear towards the garage where he had left his car, then, without waiting, drove off. They were to go to Eastgate that evening to tackle Howell; he should have converged with them on the road in a layby some miles back, but he had not been there.

'I have to talk to him,' she had told Rodney over breakfast, at which Howell did not appear. 'Not now, or he'll get cold feet and vanish, but I want to persuade him that he's got to take that clock to Taddeus at Maidment's flat. That way, either Taddeus will get away with it among the rest of the loot – which is unlikely – or it'll be found when the police pick him up. In any case, Howell will be in the clear.'

'Only a few details wrong with that. A: you don't know that Taddeus is at the flat, you only think he might have gone there. B: Howell would never have the nerve to face him. C: he's so infatuated with the clock that I doubt if he'll part with it, except to get his money back. And, D, I have forbidden you to take any more risks connected with that blasted clock or anything else.'

Doran smiled, an innocent, engaging smile. 'I won't – I promised that. I just want to make Howell see reason.'

Rodney frowned as he buttered a last piece of toast. 'Well, I don't like it, and if there's the slightest hint of trouble I shall stop the whole operation at once and drag you home. Did you know, by the way, that in our wedding ceremony you're going to promise to obey? I can see it will be necessary.'

Here was Bell House, calm and unchanged in the torpor of a dull grey Monday afternoon. With a slight shock she realized that only the day before she had expected never to see her home again.

The front garden was not over-tidy, and lacking in colour; surely there should be more flowers out. She went through the trellis gate to the back. Hammering and sawing advertised that Ozzy was working in the greenhouse. Despite the heavy, muggy atmosphere and the work he was doing he was still wearing his woolly cap and voluminous boiler-suit with a sweater underneath. He looked up glumly as she approached.

' 'Ello. Didn't expect you back yet.'

Not exactly a rousing welcome, but she could see the reason in the almost denuded rose bushes and flower beds. Ozzy had literally found a pretty picking in the second blooming of roses, to sell at his front gate, and the begonia bed looked as though every second or third cluster had been removed – so he was selling pot plants now, was he? To whom, and why, had she once described him as honest as bread?

176

'So I observe,' she said. 'What are you doing, exactly?'

'Taking down them shelves, aren't I – make more room in 'ere.'

'But you'll need them up again in a couple of months, for the stuff that's got to live here through the winter.'

'Ar. Well. Looks better without 'em. And I shan't be takin' cuttings from the . . . whatsits and . . . thingummi-bobs, not for a long time yet.'

Doran began to protest, but renewed hammering made her words inaudible. Sighing, she let herself in by the back door, which was unlocked. Either Vi or an intruder was in the house. She hoped profoundly that it was Vi, and the sound of the vacuum cleaner upstairs reassured her that it was.

Vi, at least, looked pleased when eventually she turned off the machine and saw Doran.

'Ooh! You didn't half give me a shock. Never heard you come in. You're back, then. We didn't expect you for another week, seeing it was such nice weather, but then we heard you'd a bit of trouble with the police up there, wherever it was. Nothing serious, was it?'

'Oh no, a laugh a minute, non-stop variety. Where on earth did you hear that, Vi?'

'Dunno, really – oh, may have been Lydia's Ben, going on to one of the other kids about it. Young June, that was who told me, or was it one of the Oliphants? Ben and them's always playing down the churchyard, nothing else to do in the holidays 'cept get up to mischief. How'd the vicar enjoy himself, then?'

Even Vi noticed the shock on her employer's face. 'Wasn't anyone supposed to know, then? You and him, I mean, being away together.'

'I wasn't aware that I'd told anybody. It wasn't really their business.'

Vi was suitably reproved. 'Oh. Well, I'm sorry, I'm sure. It wasn't me said anything, just . . . these things get about, you know, in a place like this.'

'Yes. Never mind, it doesn't matter. Perhaps you could go and work downstairs, now, because I'm going to unpack and have a bath.'

Mischief, indeed. *This is miching mallecho; it means mischief.* What damage have those children in the churchyard done, I wonder?

She resolved not to tell Rodney; no point in worrying him.

Rodney found Kate Oliphant in the big kitchen of the vicarage, cutting bread and butter for the family's tea. As he breezed in with apologies for returning home without warning he noticed that the smile on Kate's round rosy face did not extend to her eyes.

'That's all right,' she said, looking at the loaf, not at him. 'Vi's done your room, you can go straight up.' The atmosphere in the kitchen was not one likely to melt the butter.

'Oh, good, splendid,' he said lamely. 'Everything's gone well here?'

'Perfectly.' She buttered the last slice and arranged them all on a plate, with ostentatious care, not offering him a cup of tea or looking up again as he went out.

So she knew. That meant everybody knew. The babbling gossip of the air had cried out – Doran. Doran and he, on an illicit holiday. He wondered, with a sinking heart, how far the word would spread; Kate was a great friend of the wife of the Dean of Barminster. He resolved not to tell Doran; no point in worrying her.

Doran shut the front door and went to her car. She still intended to go to Eastgate and tackle Howell, knowing that Rodney was resistant to the idea. In the front garden of the house next door Cosmo Berg was clipping the hedge. He greeted her in the deep sexy voice she had forgotten – in fact she had forgotten his very existence.

'Hello! You weren't away for long. We thought you were going to have a real break from trade and treasures.'

'Ah. It didn't turn out quite that way.'

'Pity. I expected to see you a deep, deep Med brown by now.' His blue gaze travelled over her features caressingly, coming to rest on her lips. He had done that the first time they met, and she had thought it rather seductive, but now that she experienced it again the old trick failed to impress her. He was a phoney, a commercial traveller on a grand scale. Doubtless he had a vast repertoire of titillating stories for the benefit of his intended prey. She murmured about an appointment and started up the engine before he could try any more approaches.

Rodney was waiting where they had arranged, near the end of the vicarage garden, looking serious and preoccupied. As he joined her in the car he said, 'I suppose you intend going through with this silly project?'

'Yes, I do. And it isn't silly, just a way of getting that clock out of Howell's hair, not to mention mine. Don't worry, I shan't ask him to put his head into the lion's mouth, and I certainly shan't put mine there.'

They said very little during the journey, but, stealing a sidelong glance, she could see that he had more on his mind than their errand.

'Helena and Arline all right?'

'Fine. No complaints.'

'Good.'

Maidment's flat was in a modern block at the up-market end of the town, away from the old fishing village where most of the resident dealers lived. 'You're not going too near, I hope,' Rodney said repressively. 'Not that I believe for a moment that the man's there, but just in case he is I'd rather you didn't show yourself.'

For answer Doran turned off the seafront and drove

up a street on the opposite side from Maidment's flat. At the back of the building was a car park, shared with the next block. She stopped the Volvo at its entrance, went in, and toured the cars it held.

When she returned Rodney asked, 'What's the quest?'

'I'm looking for Maidment's car.'

'Maidment's? Not Taddeus's?'

'I explained that to you. Taddeus would be an idiot to have driven down in his own, when another was available. For goodness' sake, you haven't forgotten already?'

Rodney shook his head. 'I don't know ... it all sounded so wild. Anyway, how would you know Maidment's?'

'We all know each other's cars or vans or whatever. Can't help it, seeing them around the town so much. His is a red Escort estate, number XKO something. Right, off again.'

This time she drove to the old quarter. Under the promontory on which the ruins of Eastgate Castle stood was a car park overshadowed by a ledge of rock, and bordered by tombstones propped against what had been a churchyard wall. Doran stopped in front of it.

'What a disreputable-looking place,' Rodney said. 'How can anyone trust a car in it? You can hardly see it from the road.'

'Answer, it's got a Private notice up, if you care to look. The council lets us use it because we have to leave our wheels somewhere and they'd rather we didn't clutter up the streets except for loading and unloading. As you may note, hardly any of the build-ings round here have garages – they weren't exactly prolific in the eighteenth century. The general public do sneak in sometimes but there's always someone coming and going, and we slap warning notices on strange cars, like *People round here are dead criminal and collect car radios,* with a skull and crossbones decoration. You'd be surprised how they take notice of it and shift.'

Her search was short. Returning, she pointed triumphantly to the red estate car parked retiringly beneath the cliff-jut.

'There it is. Didn't I tell you it would be?'

'So Taddeus is at the flat,' Rodney said heavily. 'You're not going there, you know. I won't have it, and I don't want any arguments from you.'

'Won't be any. I promised, didn't I. Stop nagging.'

Howell's cottage was called Reefers, a name which Doran pointed out as highly felicitous. Rodney seemed not to find it amusing. The bell, an ancient iron one, jangled twice before Howell answered the door. His welcome was tepid.

'Oh. Didn't expect you, did I.'

'Well, you failed to meet up with us as arranged, so here we are.' Doran pushed past him into the spacious parlour which had been created by the knocking down of a wall between the front and back of the cottage. It was furnished with exquisite taste in a manner which only just avoided being high camp. Victorian and Georgian, like righteousness and peace, kissed each other, setting off each other's charms in amity. Over the elegant duck's-nest fireplace a pair of early girandoles winked back coloured sparks from their lustres, a portrait of Andrew's handsome great-grandmother looked majestically out from a frame which incorporated mother of pearl, plaster fruit and lace. There was a great deal of lace elsewhere in the room, draped on a Sheraton chaise longue and a walnut square piano. A bracket filled with 'twenties cups and saucers hung above a graceful bust of the young Marie Antoinette. The whole effect was pretty and witty and uplifting to the spirits, if one felt like it.

Rodney did not. When Doran had settled on the

181

chaise longue he sat beside her, very close and near the edge, ready to jump up if she were menaced.

Andrew wore a pale blue Japanese robe and there was glitter powder on his hair. He was nervous and could easily have been cross. Howell put out whatever he had been smoking and abandoned a can of beer on the veined marble mantelpiece. The daring post-Morris wallpaper in peacock blues outstared them all.

Then Doran said: 'Taddeus is here, Howell – hiding up in Vic's flat. He's on the run and he's got a lot of stuff with him. I want you to give him the clock back.'

Howell stared and gasped, shaking his head unbelievingly.

'He's not forgotten it, you can bet. When he sold it to you he didn't know this was going to happen. Now it has, all he wants is to get away with as much as he can. He's a bit mad, and money-madness is part of it – I ought to know, I've seen him in action, so to speak. He adores beautiful things, worships them – and you didn't pay him the full price of the clock, did you?'

'No, but . . .'

'How much did you pay him?'

'Seven thou'. Cheque and cash.'

'And what was he asking?'

'Fifteen.'

'So you owe him eight, and he won't have overlooked that little detail. He's going to skip across the water any time now, possibly without the loot. Cecile's French contacts will fix that, and he'll need all the money and saleable goods he can get his hands on to set up over there, because he daren't go back to Gloucestershire. Now, why don't you wrap the clock up, go to Vic's flat, put it down outside the door, knock and leave?'

Andrew, pink with agitation, was trying to speak. Howell laid a restraining hand on his arm, saying, 'Dunno about Taddeus being mad – *you* are.'

'No, I'm being perfectly reasonable. You needn't pay

182

the balance – as the clock was stolen it would be immoral to give him any more for it. Just let him have it back and get it off our hands. You've had your fun with it, haven't you!'

'Fun! If that's your idea of fun, mate, 'tisn't mine. 'Sides . . . '

Andrew ceased his impersonation of a goldfish and interrupted. 'Lay off him! You don't understand. Just stop yacking and let him tell you.'

Howell drew a deep breath. 'In the first place, I don't believe Tony Taddeus is in Eastgate – bilge. You want to come down to earth, gal, and stop dreamin'. In the second place . . . '

The doorbell jangled. Andrew said something violent, strode to the door and threw it open.

Tony Taddeus entered, pushed the door shut, and surveyed the assembled company with a pleasant smile. 'What luck! All at home. Well, Mr Evans, we meet again – how fortunate that you aren't ex-directory.'

Rodney leapt up and stood in front of Doran. Andrew shrank into the corner of the chaise longue. Howell said hoarsely, '*Warra teg!* You *are* here, then.'

'Looks as if I'm here, doesn't it, though I'm not sure how you found out.'

'It was me, actually,' Doran said, emerging from behind Rodney. She was very frightened but determined to appear calm; it was when Cecile had fought him that he had turned violent and stabbed her.

'How very clever.' Taddeus sounded as if he meant it. 'Brains as well as beauty. And you got out of Stanisley House quite safely – well done. I suppose they found Cecile quite soon after I left?'

'Quite soon. They're looking for your car, not Vic's, that's how . . . '

Rodney snapped at her, 'Be quiet, I'll handle this.' But Taddeus had moved into the other half of the room and was standing in front of a table which bore an assortment of small clocks. 'What a pretty collection, and so varied. I love the late balloon, and the cartel, and I absolutely covet the early iron with the foliot. Can't be Tudor, can it? Though I'd swear it is, and if so, I wonder how you got hold of it? Better not ask, perhaps. But I don't see mine. Come on, where is it?'

'It's not exactly yours, it's Lady Timberlake's,' Doran said. Taddeus shot her a look that was not at all admiring, and moved to tower over Howell. 'I don't want any playing about,' he said. 'I've come for my property – mine because you didn't finish paying for it, remember? I want it, and I want the balance of the cash. Don't bother about a cheque – that wouldn't be much use where I'm going. I'll take all the cash you have in the house, and what your guests have on them. Coins thankfully accepted.' He held out one large hand, the left; the other was in his pocket. Rodney's eyes were on it.

'If you've got your celebrated knife there,' he said, 'I'd think again about using it. We're four to one, and you're more used to dealing with a woman on her own, I believe.'

Taddeus ignored him, addressing Howell. 'Come on. I want the clock. Where it is?'

Howell gulped. 'I haven't got it any more.'

'You *what*?'

'I . . . I found a buyer. He asked to have it quick, so . . .'

Taddeus picked him up by the open collar of his shirt and shook him violently, making sounds which Doran supposed were what was meant by the expression swearing horribly. Howell seemed to be choking and Andrew shrieked, clawing ineffectually at Taddeus's arm. Taddeus shook him off and produced from his right pocket a small gun.

'This isn't a toy, it's a Nazi buckle pistol, and it fires, as you'll find out if your friend doesn't tell me within ten seconds where my clock is.' He pressed the gun into Andrew's ribs, while Howell shouted between gasps.

'Put me down, you bugger! I can't . . . I can't . . .'

Rodney pushed Doran away and advanced on Taddeus, whose back was towards him and whose whole attention was taken up in throttling Howell. Rodney struck him squarely at the base of the skull with the carborundum paperweight. He fell without a sound and lay inert on the flower-embroidered carpet. Doran noted automatically that it was hand-knotted, made in Axminster, and probably very early Victorian.

'I hope I haven't killed him,' Rodney said, 'but if I have it can't be helped. Where do you keep your telephone, Howell?'

Police stations are traditionally quiet on Monday evenings, and Eastgate was no exception. The statements of the four shaken people from Reefers were taken down at leisure, from Doran and Rodney at length. Howell and Andrew were judged to be still in shock, making little sense. After a hurried consultation before the arrival of the police Doran had made them promise not to mention the clock, though Rodney protested that to leave it out of their accounts was dishonest, not to say dangerous.

'If we don't tell them they won't know,' she said. 'Call the whole thing a revenge attempt, Taddeus trying to get his own back on us for foiling him. Only we must all tell the same story.' She outlined it, a brief and simple account which could be checked with the Cotswold police.

'Then, when they let us go, Howell and I will get the clock, return the money and give the clock back to Lady Timberlake. Who's got it now, Howell?'

'A prince,' said the miserable Howell. 'Do I *have* to give the money back? A whole seven thou'?'

'Of course. What prince, and where?'

'A sort of Arabian guy, loaded, he is, bought Blandish Park.'

'That great Sussex place? He *must* be loaded.'

'Stinking with it. Oil. Got a harem, too, I shouldn't wonder. They frisk you like the Customs before they let you in – after the telly-scanner's passed you OK. Scared me stupid. But he was wild to get his hands on the East, sort of petting it like it was a little puppy. Suppose it's the brass they go for, nice and shiny, it attracts them, see.'

'You're thinking of backward natives in some remote jungle, Howell – if there are any left – not Eton-educated royalty. Never mind. I'll sort it out when this lot's over.'

The police appeared satisfied with the four separate yet tallying accounts. Detective-Inspector McMurdo of the CID, a Scot of high principles, approved of Rodney's detailed version. He wondered how a minister of the Gospel came to be mixed up in such dealings. He was pleased to be able to convey a good report of Taddeus from the hospital to which he had been taken, unconscious: the X-ray showed nothing likely to result in death, paralysis, or brain damage, and the patient was already coming round.

'Thank God,' said Rodney.

Doran said, 'I bet he won't mention the clock.' Light-headed with reaction from the evening, she murmured,

> *'You intoxified brute – you insensible block –*
> *Look at the Clock! do! look at the Clock!'*

Howell looked pleased, for the first time. 'I know that, you said some of it to me once. About some Welsh guy, Pryce, that was it, used to sing a lot.' He demonstrated.

> *'Chwyth y rhewynt dros ye bryniau*
> *Gyda thoriad qwawr y dydd . . . '*

186

'Thank you,' Doran said hastily. 'Don't let them think we're drunk.'

The prince of Blandish Park, known to close friends as Harry because part of his sequence of names was Harith, was certainly not a backward native, and his alma mater was not in doubt. His black and white chequered headdress emphasized his strong resemblance to the late Rudolph Valentino, with whom Doran had fallen in love during a film festival which featured *Blood and Sand*. His long sloe eyes, olive skin and sensuous lips added up to quite something, she concluded, and when he declared himself anxious to please her in any way she fully believed him. She was glad she had left Howell in the car.

But at the mention of the clock the beautiful sloe eyes visibly moistened with melancholy.

'My dear Miss Fairweather. How I wish I could give it back to you. Of course I would, no question. Only – I haven't got it. A great friend of mine who was staying here recently took a violent fancy to it, and – well, in my part of the world it's the custom to present a guest with anything he, or she of course, admires openly. So, rather reluctantly, I said, "Take it." What else could I do?'

'What, indeed. The only trouble is, it wasn't Mr Evans's to sell – in fact, it was stolen property.' She sketched a few details from the events of the past week. 'So you see. I've managed not to mention it to the police, because I don't want Mr Evans to get into trouble. Bent dealers aren't popular with the law, and some of the odium would rub off on me.'

His Highness nodded slowly, and strengthened the gin and tonic in her glass and his own, and leaned gracefully back against cushions. Doran thought of attar of roses and bulbuls and Byronic reveries. There was a subtle, delicious perfume in the otherwise wholly

187

English drawing room looking out on a smiling Sussex park, where distant race-horses grazed, and it was all very pleasant and unlike her recent experiences.

'I'll telephone, of course,' said Prince Harry. 'God only knows where my friend is by now, but I have a contact in New York who might just be able to get in touch. As soon as I tell him what's happened he'll find a way of getting the clock back here, and you shall have it at the first possible moment. All right?'

'All right. Shall I give you the cheque now? It's made out, with today's date.'

He smiled, a slow seductive smile. 'That's so kind, wonderfully honest of you. But I couldn't – I simply wouldn't dream of it. Not yet, at any rate. Not until I can put the clock into your hands.'

Doran struggled to her feet from the luxurious couch, inelegantly. He followed suit, and stood close, looking into her eyes with a gaze of penetrating sweetness which had a curious effect on her. She told herself not to be silly. She had, she was sure, just been conned in the sublimest possible way, but it had been worth it for the experience; and now Howell would not have to pay back the seven thousand.

'About the old lady,' Prince Harry said as they went to the door. 'Don't think of driving all that way yourself, when the clock eventually finds its way back here. I shall personally see to it. My chauffeur will quite enjoy the drive, I expect.'

Don't he wish he may get it, thought Doran, in the words of the Reverend R. H. Barham, who had been very far from her mind in the perfumed halls of Blandish Park.

Ah, well. Back to normality, and whatever was going to happen next.

CHAPTER THIRTEEN

Wedding-fingers are sweet pretty things

Abbotsbourne was in the grip of mid-August fever. An interlude of typical English summer weather – heavy grey low-lying cloud and unpleasantly becalmed air – had passed, giving way to continuous sunshine with temperatures reaching the nineties. Ozzy was unusually contented, plying the watering can and the hose liberally over a few plants which needed it and many which did not. At least he knew what he was doing and it kept him from brooding on the bunches of asters he might have been picking and selling.

The Rose Reviv'd seethed with visitors, from before opening time, when they gathered on the benches in the forecourt and waited, until long after closing time, when they returned to the forecourt and made a great deal of noise. The annexe at the back of the building, completed by the Bellacres in spring, was constantly full; buxom Rosie lost half a stone rushing to and from the new rooms to the kitchens.

The Feathers, a plainer and homelier pub, did a roaring trade, its patrons spilling out on to the pavement and into the car park at the side. Sam Eastry and young Constable Liddell were more than once called to incidents between over-stimulated customers, and Sam was summoned to a case of alleged shoplifting at the general store which sold an enormous variety of useless articles. A tourist from London was noticed by

Miss Tite, the owner, wandering about the shop clutching a pottery group of a mother pig bathing its piglets. When the woman left the shop, having bought a daily paper, the pig family was nowhere to be seen. When Sam arrived on his Honda Miss Tite was in the street haranguing the customer, who was in tears.

'You took it, I saw you!'

'I didn't. I never.'

'You did – search her, Sam.'

'I'm afraid I can't do that, Miss Tite, it's not allowed. But if you wouldn't mind turning out your pockets and your bag, madam, we can settle things nicely.'

Protesting, she obeyed. From the depths of her raffia bag the blue-eyed pigs emerged, smilingly unconscious of the stir they were causing. The customer sat down on the step of the shop and sobbed loudly. 'Now, now,' said Sam.

'I told you,' exulted Miss Tite. 'Go on, arrest her.'

'Er, not without a charge, Miss Tite.'

'I'm charging her, then. Get on with it!'

Sam took her aside and murmured that a public arrest would attract a lot of notice and be bad for business, and in any case the shop was full of other customers – some of them might be merely gawping, but others could well be filling their own pockets, if so minded. Miss Tite saw reason, and Sam issued a gentle but firm warning that a repetition of the offence, etcetera, and that the article must be paid for.

'I 'ate the thing, I don't want it,' sniffed the customer. 'Didn't know I 'ad it in me 'and, did I.' She threw three pound coins down on the counter. 'There you are, you old bat, use it to get yer broomstick polished. And this is the last time you'll see me in this rotten village, I can tell yer.'

Sam looked after her, shaking his head. A plump little female traffic warden approached him, notebook in hand, her face all one beam.

190

''Morning, Sam. My word, trade's brisk today. Haven't this lot seen a double yellow line before? Oh, and a Cortina's run into the back of a Triumph, round the corner in Cow Lane – better see if you can trace the owner, and when you do I'll have him, he's fifteen minutes over time.'

At the Saturday cricket match all was peace and decorum. Abbotsbourne First Eleven were playing Great Markham, a team from the other side of Barminster. It was a new fixture, and the home side rejoiced to find Great Markham's bowling nervous and terse, but limited – as, Sam recalled, Sherlock Holmes had remarked about the vocabulary of *Bradshaw*. Bob Woods, opening for Abbotsbourne, was battling as though the ball were under orders to fly wherever he directed it, especially over the small pavilion, where it was trained to land in a neighbouring garden for six. He would be in need of the large tea which Vi Small and his wife Barbary were preparing, sandwiches, scones, bread and butter with home-made lemon curd, and Vi's walnut cake.

Outside the pavilion young Donald Woods was being minded by a tiny, ancient Anglo-Indian woman, Greta Singh, his parents' friend and his resident nanny. Sam remembered last summer, when Greta had tragically lost her old husband, and Abbotsbourne had nearly lost its cricket ground, all through a man who – what was Holmes's description? – *tortured the soul and wrung the nerves* as a form of devilish fun.

Doran was sitting on the far side of the field, alone. Her face wore its lost look; like, Sam told himself in a flight of poetic fancy, a flower plucked and left to droop in a vase without water. Her holiday had not done her much good, and small wonder, from what she had told him and what he had picked up at Eastgate.

She had got into something too deep for her: *these*

are deep waters, Doran. But with luck her part in it was over. Taddeus would eventually come up for trial, and Sam hoped earnestly that she would not be damaged by the revival of all that grimness, or by anything which might emerge in the evidence.

But he knew by instinct that something nearer home was pulling her down. Not Rodney's involvement in the Cotswold murders and their sequel, but the fact that Abbotsbourne knew about their having been away together. Gossiping old-fashioned Abbotsbourne, you could rely on it to make the most and the worst of something like that. The stories had come to Sam by way of Lydia.

'Staying at a pub as man and wife . . . travelling in her car, while his was at the Downs Service Station out of sight . . . telephoning here to get you to vouch for him, and giving a false name . . . Oh, Sam, where has it all come from? I'm sure I never said a word about that phone call, or any of what you and I talked about. I couldn't have done, I wouldn't. Who did?'

Sam found out. His expression was grim as he told her.

'It was our Ben. I had a sort of inkling, and finally I got it out of him. He was around that morning, in and out, and put two and two together. Then William Oliphant said something that tied up, and between them they got a story together about the vicar running off with Miss Fairweather and getting arrested. Before long they were all giggling about it.'

Lydia was furious, and said so. 'A policeman's son! He knows better than that. Wait till I tackle him. There's nothing ever wrong with children that a good smacked bottom won't cure, my granny used to say.'

'He's too old for that, Lyd. It wouldn't do any good. He's at a silly age, and the other kids egg him on to tell things, you know what they are. I've ticked him off, don't worry. But the harm's done now, and the more either of us says, the worse it will get. Let it be.'

'All very well. But secrets, and specially those sort of secrets, spreading out of this house . . . What would the superintendent say if it got back to him?'

'Let's hope it won't. I tell you what, Lyd, if it'll make you feel any better – it wasn't just Ben started these stories. Things sort of get into the air in a country place – walls have ears, and all that. And it was to be expected, wasn't it? Everyone's always known Doran and the vicar were – well, fond of each other. So when they're both away at the same time, people say . . . what they've been saying.'

Lydia brooded. 'William Oliphant, too. He's younger than Ben, but quite old enough to know better. A policeman's lad and a vicar's, tattling like a couple of old women! Whatever next?'

Rodney was unpleasantly aware of the tattle. Before he had gone away his small attic room had been a refuge of peace. Now he felt like an intruder in his own home. David, the Oliphant's fourteen-year-old, had been using it for a blissful week as a studio for his hi-fi gear, mixing imaginary record tracks with his brother William's assistance, well out of his mother's way. Now he had been evicted, obliged to take down his cherished pop posters.

'Mum says they're obscene,' he grumbled, drawing-pins in his mouth. 'I don't think so, do you?'

Rodney surveyed the blown-up record sleeve still on the wall. If not actually obscene, it was certainly far from decorous. 'I'd say it was more ugly than anything. But my taste isn't yours, David. I can see what your mother means. Sorry to turn you out, though.'

' 's all right.' But David's tone said that it was not.

Father Oliphant seemed unaffected by the atmosphere, and was perfectly cordial to Rodney. 'I can tell you how much I've enjoyed my time here. Lovely church, lovely people. Full pews and happy faces, that's what I like to see, and I've had 'em for every service – well, not the 7.30, of course, but even that's been enjoyable, getting up early in this beautiful place – the morning light on the Downs, and the scent of roses from your garden – a bit better than my little suburban St John's was, I can tell you.'

Rodney forebore to say how much he himself disliked getting up early, however beautiful the place. 'You don't mind having to use the ASB?'* he asked.

'Good gracious no, I love it. Why some of us insist on sticking to that other archaic stuff I'll never know. Modern language for modern times, that's what I say, and the same goes for the new Bible. Oh – but didn't I hear something about you and the Bishop, and retaining Matins?'

'Yes. I do like the Cranmer liturgy, as it happens; and Bloody Mary did burn the man alive for standing by it. Somehow I feel it shouldn't be cast aside all that lightly.'

'Hm. I wonder if your younger parishioners agree with you, entirely?'

'I don't know. I've never asked them.'

Father Oliphant shook his head. 'I wish you and I could work together, my dear Rodney. I think we might learn something from each other.'

Kate Oliphant hardly spoke to Rodney. In her eyes he had disgraced himself thoroughly, and was condemned without a trial. Herself the daughter of a bishop who, four centuries earlier, would cheerfully have burnt anyone alive for disagreeing with his views, she was a woman who carried principle to extremes. She had said nothing directly to her children, leaving them to pick up vibrations from her tone and manner. They were quick enough to do so. Rodney fancied that even the seven-year-old twins, Martha and Mary, looked askance at him.

*Alternative Service Book

It was when one of his most faithful parishoners, the widowed, pious Mrs Lewes, deliberately crossed the High Street to avoid him, that he came to a decision. He got out the car and drove to Eastgate, at a faster speed than his normal one. If he were caught by a police patrol car it would be just one more serious crime against his name.

Doran was alone in the shop, washing china in the sink at the back.

'Oh, hello,' she said brightly, emerging. 'Just looking round, are you, or can I interest you in anything particular? This, for instance.' She fished a plate out of the water. 'Scene of Bishop Bonner, the well-known Hammer of Heretics, binding a prisoner's hands before sending him to the stake. Unusual, isn't it?'

'Horrible. It reminds me of a conversation I had recently. Look, I didn't drop in for idle chat about Bonner or anything else, and I'm sorry you're cross with me. I did warn you I wasn't exactly going to cling round you just at the moment.'

Very carefully Doran dried and polished the plate. 'You did, and I do understand about letting things cool down in Abbotsbourne. But you could have come here before. I think it's a bit poor, frankly.'

'I'm sorry, darling, I'm very, very sorry.' He put his arms round her and would not be shaken off. 'I felt I had to – take the temperature of the place, find out just how it reacted to the gossip. Being seen with you would only have made matters worse.'

'They're bad, then?'

'Awful.' He told her of his cold-shouldering at the vicarage. 'And now even Mrs Lewes – and I thought she was one who'd never desert Mr Micawber, but she has. What's it been like for you?'

Doran shrugged. 'At first I was obviously Typhoid Mary, but then curiosity got too much for them and they started engaging me in conversation, looking me up and down all the time, to find out what a Ruined

195

Maid's actually like, I suppose. I didn't give them any change – *One's pretty lively when ruined, said she.* Women are news, aren't they. It's all made me feel like using words that would send one of Howell's Cardiff sailor friends reeling back with shock. And admiration, possibly.'

'But you didn't. Nor did I – I've been as mild as the milk that dews the soft whisker of the new-weaned kitten.'

'Very nice. Not, I take it, original?'

'Barham yet again. Preface to the second edition of the *Legends*, with a wholly fictitious drawing of Tappington Everard. Listen: we're going to get married.'

Doran's hands flew to her cheeks. 'Married? What, now?'

'As soon as I can get a special licence. We won't need banns, and we could do it next Saturday, with all the other lovebirds. Father Oliphant will still be in charge, and I know he'd rejoice to be the one to make an honest man of me. Never mind about Helena for the moment – she's got Arline. It's the only thing to do, Doran. I know it's bending over to satisfy convention and absolutely ridiculous in this day and age, but the circumstances are a bit special, you must admit. After that, they'll stop whispering, you'll see. I'm not chicken, I can take it, but I don't think the poor old Church can. See?'

'Yes. And you're right. But I've got nothing to wear.' She caught his eye. 'And no, I didn't have virgin white in mind.'

'A good few of the brides I've married have carried extra-large bouquets for all too obvious reasons – which won't, of course, be yours.'

Doran crossed her fingers behind her back. 'Not unless Science is the fairy tale Tennyson thought it was, and how would he know?'

'Harriet Vane was married in gold brocade designed by Worth.'

'Harriet Vane was also dark and dramatic-looking – and the circumstances were a little different. Never mind, it's fairly unimportant. What about . . . '

The shop-bell jangled and the head of a small monkey-faced man peered in. 'Wotcher, Dore.'

'Oh – Bill. Er . . . '

'I got a coupla nice boxes for you to look through, a few choice bits in 'em, very tasty, very sweet. Picked 'em up here, there and everywhere, like a little sparrer flittin' from twig to twig. Where do I put 'em down? Anythin' wrong, Dore?'

'Oh, no – not at all, far from it. Bill, could you just give me five minutes? This is Rodney Chelmarsh, by the way, Bill Jackson. We need to sort something out, very quickly – do you mind?'

'My darlin', it'll be a pleasure. I'll go down the Port Arms and have one, if you like, come back later.'

'No, don't do that. Just go and sit in the van. And Bill – you can call me Dore today, if you like, and I won't object.' She sent him a brilliant smile.

'You won't? Cor. I know you 'ate it and I always forgets. What was it you said once – I could call you Dore when it was your birfday. Is that it, then?'

'Not exactly, but you're near.'

When he had gone Rodney said, 'I've an idea. Can you shut up shop for lunch?'

'When I've seen Bill's bits and pieces, yes. He's my runner for the London markets.'

'Because *I* can go down the Port Arms and have one, then come back for you and we'll go for a mystery tour, with some sandwiches and a couple of bottles. Come to think, I'll get them at the pub, Right?'

'Right. A Magical Mystery Tour? No.' Doran shivered. 'I sang all the numbers from that album when I was in that place. I never want to hear "The Fool on the Hill" again, ever.'

'Don't worry, I won't inflict it on you. See you.'

*　*　*

The car crawled respectfully through what had been the heart of wartime air defences, wound its way up twisting lanes, overhung with trees which met, forming long aisles of shadowy green, then swooped down through woods into a valley, climbed again, navigated a wide corner and halted.

'Look down to the left,' Rodney said.

It lay far below them in a meadow-valley, a fine comfortable ancient house neighboured by modern farm buildings and backed by a wooded hill.

'Tappington Everard. The real one, the Ingoldsbys' country home. The picture in the *Legends* is a house farther up the road – he was having a little joke with his readers, pretending Tappington was much grander than it was. One would hardly call this road a beautiful green lane, as he did – it was, then, of course, two hundred years ago, when Barham was a boy, but he'd know the house. I just thought we ought to come and see it, having been Mr and Mrs Barham so recently.'

'I love it. I loved being Mrs Barham. I shall love being Mrs Chelmarsh. I love you. And I'm starving – are we going to picnic here?'

'Not if you want to survive long enough to become Mrs Chelmarsh,' said Rodney, as a gigantic Dutch transport roared past them, narrowly missing the car.

'Let's go and find a sequestered nook, if there are any left; if not, an unsequestered layby. I've a lot to do this afternoon.'

The first thing he did was to seek out Father Oliphant, picking late strawberries in the kitchen garden. 'Good afternoon, Father,' Rodney greeted him. 'Will you marry me? If you know what I mean.'

Oliphant dropped the basket and stood amazed, strawberries spilling round his feet.

'My dear boy. You and ...? Bless me! What a delightful ... Of course, of course. When? How soon?'

'As soon as I can get a Special from Barminster – I'm going there now. We thought perhaps – next Saturday afternoon?'

The old clergyman shook his head. 'With all those couples? It's like a sausage machine. No, for a special licence we'll have a special wedding – what about half-past eleven on Saturday morning, then we can have a jolly lunch afterwards? I always enjoy a nuptial lunch, so much more fun than afternoon tea.'

'Yes. Deeply boring, afternoon tea. But do you think Kate will be exactly geared to a jolly lunch? I've detected a certain frost in her attitude to me, and she may well regard this as a shotgun wedding, which it isn't. Would you mind awfully if we make it the Rose?'

'Mm ... you have a point. I'm sure she'll come round, women always do at weddings. But make it the Rose, just to avoid any shadow on the proceedings, however slight. The children won't be allowed in, of course, but they can have whatever they're drinking outside. We *are* all invited, aren't we?'

They were all invited. Martha and Mary, suddenly recovering from the suspicions imparted by their mother, volunteered as bridesmaids in twin party frocks. Rodney dispensed with a best man, as, he pointed out, Royalty had set a precedent by doing, though Howell had magnanimously offered himself in that capacity – but then, as he agreed, he was Chapel, and it wouldn't have done. Kate Oliphant, as her husband had predicted, could not resist attending, or warming into affability. The family terrier remained at home.

Doran delighted Howell by inviting Andrew – he

had, after all, been through a bad evening with them – and all her dealer friends from Eastgate and district. Many Abbotsbournians who were not invited turned up at the church, including the Bergs from Magnolia House. Handsome in designer clothes, seated on the bride's friends' side, Richenda and Cosmo surveyed their next-door neighbour and her consort with feelings the congregation could not have guessed at: there, they reflected separately, were two that got away . . .

The Woods were present, Greta Singh with them, wearing a festive gilt-spangled crimson sari, Rupert Wylie the young estate agent, who counted Doran one of his few amorous failures; with him was his own intended bride, a spectacularly beautiful earl's daughter closely resembling in many points a Palomino filly. Vi was resplendent in petunia crimplene. Ozzy wore his only suit. Even Marcia Fawkes and Stella Meeson were there, having heard of the wedding through their grapevine, Stella wilder in appearance than ever, clad in bright purple from head to foot.

In the ringing chamber Sam was in charge of his team – three regulars and two deputies – to ring the happiest wedding-chime of his life. He thought of the horrors that had been told to him, of the perilous evening at Eastgate, and the murderer now awaiting trial and, Sam hoped, a life sentence. He thought of Doran – like a daughter, she had always seemed to him (hadn't Holmes said that of some female character?) and, unlike his own daughter, she had survived.

Rodney turned, as the organist began whatever they had chosen instead of the hackneyed Wedding March. He was as nervous as though he had never attended a wedding before. Up the aisle, on the arm of Ernest Tilman, the bank manager, Doran was coming towards him, a Dulac figure of fairy tale, in a simple medieval gown of grey-blue silk shot with threads of pink and gold, full-sleeved from the elbows, modestly high-necked and girdled with a gilt cord from which hung a pomander. On the back of her curls she wore a Juliet cap of jewels sewn on net.

She joined him, and looked up at him, smiling, and he saw that the jewels were theatrical paste, the gown old, threadbare in places. He had never in all his years seen a more romantically beautiful bride.

From that moment neither remembered anything clearly, except that Rodney recalled that Father Oliphant had kindly used the old form of service. When they came to themselves the reception at the Rose was in full cry, a confusion of handshakes, kisses, laughter, champagne, and presents laid out on a miniature snooker table. Doran unwrapped Howell's while he watched eagerly. It was a fan, by Brunelleschi, made in the second decade of the twentieth century, an infinitely delicate thing of paper, on which a gauze-clad, turbaned girl gazed at a peacock, both drawn in pale gold, vieux rose and black. Doran's collection of fans was a personal passion, outside the area of dealing.

'Oh, Howell! How did you know? I've got nothing like it. It's the rarest, most precious thing. Oh, you're wonderful!' She hugged and kissed him, and, for the first time in living memory, he blushed.

'Well, you're not so bad yourself, gal. Got me out of a tight corner, didn't you, with that flamin' clock.'

'Let's not congratulate ourselves too soon – it may catch up with us yet. Wouldn't it have been marvellous if the Prince had sent it as a wedding present?'

'Some hopes.'

'Some hopes. What did you say, Rodney?'

'I asked you where the heck you got that dress.'

'Oh, that was Meg.' She indicated the female half of a married couple of dealers. 'She sells a lot of old tat, but she does collect stage costume as well. This is a Juliet. It came from the old Worthing Theatre before they pulled it down. Heaven knows how it's held together this long, it's almost in rags. But I thought it was just right, somehow, picturesque but not gaudy. Don't start on Romeo, though – you've had so much champagne you could go on and on.'

'I wasn't going to mention Romeo. I was going to say, A lovelier bride, in her degree, Man's eye might never hope to see Than darling, bonnie Maud Ingoldsby . . .'

Bell House was very quiet, when they got home. There was no question of their going away for a honeymoon – they'd just had one, they agreed. A large, curiously shaped parcel waited in the hall.

The wrappings at last fell away. Doran was looking at the dummy-board figure she had coveted at Broadway, the little Queen Anne girl in her stiff gown and lace fontange.

'Bridegroom's present to bride,' Rodney said.

'I wanted it so. I don't know what to say . . .'

'Then don't.' When he at last detached himself from her he said, '*This* came by the first post – marvellous timing. I ought to have told you then, in case you wanted to call the whole thing off, but I couldn't bring myself to spoil the day. Make any comments you like. We'll talk about different housing arrangements, if that helps. I just don't know. Here. Read it.'

The letter was written in a bold heavy hand.

Dear Rod, I thought you ought to know that I won't be working for you after next week. I met this guy Steve from Wanganui, not far off my part of the world, and we got on just famously. I think this is it, Rod, but anyway we're teaming up to see how it goes. Hope you get somebody else to cope with Helena, she's a right little problem, a real pain, but it just needs a firm hand. We'll be back

*on Sunday night, you can dock my wages instead
of notice if you like, anyway see you then,
Best, Arline.*

'*Well!*' Doran gasped. 'Of all the effrontery!
Wretched, tiresome, bloody girl! What are you going
to do?'

'What do *you* think?'

She thought. 'Manage. Make the best of it. I can
face it now. I'm strong.'

'Sure that's not just euphoria talking?'

'No. No, I'm sure of it. I don't know why I was so
silly and cowardly before – lack of confidence, I
suppose. Worse things than Helena have happened
this last week.'

'That's my good wife. Thank you for taking it like
that. I could hardly believe you would: thank God.
Oh – and something else I have to break to you.
Again, I should have said this before, but I was afraid
of rocking the boat, and I've still got some thinking to
do, anyway.'

'Good gracious. What have you done?'

'It's more what I want to do. I think I want to get
out of the Church. I feel I've had enough of it, the in-
fighting and the way I look at certain things. It's
become Me versus Them. I think the stark reality of
the Oliphants had something to do with it. They'll
win, you know, these Alternative Service people, I
can see it coming.'

'But we had the proper service today, not the
souped-up one.'

'We were lucky, probably one of the last of the few.
In a year or two there'll be no ritual, no robes, no
solemnity and awe left: we'll all be sitting round on
cushions drinking Foster's and chatting extempore,
like. But my darling, you were expecting to be a
vicar's lady. Would you mind if you weren't?'

'Mind? Not one bit – on the contrary. I'd have been

203

rotten at it, and I think that was nagging at me, as well as the Helena thing. No. What you want is very important indeed, and I'm absolutely with you. But what will you do, instead?'

'I don't know. I know what I mustn't do, and that includes a lot: I don't know yet what I must, or could do. I'll be shown, directed, don't you worry. Meanwhile, it's a beautiful afternoon, and still our wedding day. There sits a bird on yonder tree More fond than cushat dove: There sits a bird on yonder tree And sings to me of love. Come into the garden, Mrs Barham: for such you will always be to me.'

THE END

Malice Domestic
by Mollie Hardwick

Nothing ever happened in Abbotsbourne.
Doran Fairweather — twenty-six and pretty with it — sold her
antiques, flirted with the vicar, and enjoyed her calm existence
at Bell House. Then Mr Mumbray moved into the The Oaks.

It wasn't just that he looked like Erich von Stroheim that made
everyone uneasy — but with his arrival things began to happen
— Marcia Fawkes took to drink, the Haydon-Trees moved
swiftly out of the village without saying goodbye, and a
teenager committed suicide for no apparent reason. Leonard
Mumbray seemed to carry a miasma of evil around with him
that affected everyone, so when he was murderd no one felt at
all sorry.

But Doran felt there was more to come, more to the murder
than everyone thought. She determined to catch the murderer,
not realising that she could well be the next victim.

0552 132357

A Late Phoenix
by Catherine Aird

Three decades have passed since a German bomb flattened the houses in Lamb Lane — three decades, and then a workman's pickaxe uncovers an old macabre mystery, the skeleton of a girl, an unborn child, and a bullet. Detective Inspector C. D. Sloan's uncanny instincts began to detect a crime not quite as old as it appeared to be — a crime that might explode again into murder.

A Classic Case of Murder

0552 127949

The Complete Steel
by Catherine Aird

Ornum House was open to the public on Wednesdays, Saturdays, and Sundays. Mrs Fisher, dragging her unwilling family around the Stately Home had never intended to go down to the dungeons and armoury, but when her son Michael went missing she knew that that was where he was likely to be. She caught him just in time, struggling to open a standing suit of armour.

'Look, Mum,' he shouted, wrenching at the vizor, and at that moment he managed to lift it.

A face stared back. It was a modern face, a twentieth century face, the face of Mr Meredith, Librarian of Ornum House. And he was dead.

A Classic Case of Murder

0552 127922

Wycliffe and the Schoolgirls
by W. J. Burley

First Debbie Joyce, a cabaret singer, was found strangled. A week later, in the same city, Nurse Elaine Bennett was murdered in the same way and the alarm went out — a psychopathic killer is on the loose.

But Wycliffe was not convinced. Slowly he dug into the past of the murdered girls — a past that took him back to a school holiday and the persecution of one particular child by 'the group'. Was someone working off an old revenge — and how many more women would die because of a cruel schoolgirl joke?

0552 128058

Wycliffe and the Pea Green Boat
by W. J. Burley

Tragedy seemed to stalk the Tremain family. Sidney Tremain had hanged himself for no obvious reason. His son, Morley, had had the misfortune to fall in love with a girl who slept around — and get convicted of killing her. And now Cedric Tremain was charged with murdering his wealthy father by blowing up his boat.

Chief Superintendent Wycliffe knew something was wrong, knew that the apparently cut and dried case wasn't what it appeared to be. Carefully he cast his bait — and waited for the real killer to surface.

0552 12804X

A SELECTED LIST OF CRIME TITLES
AVAILABLE FROM CORGI BOOKS